THE
RESURRECTION
FIELDs

Also by Brian Keaney:

The Promises of Dr. Sigmundus, Book One: *The Hollow People*

The Promises of Dr. Sigmundus, Book Two: *The Cracked Mirror*

THE PROMISES OF DR. SIGMUNDUS

BOOK THREE

BRIAN KEANEY

ALFRED A. KNOPF
NEW YORK

THIS IS A BORZOI BOOK PUBLISHED BY ALFRED A. KNOPF

Visit us on the Web! www.randomhouse.com/teens

Educators and librarians, for a variety of teaching tools, visit us at
www.randomhouse.com/teachers

The Library of Congress has cataloged the hardcover edition of this work as follows:
Keaney, Brian.
[Promises of Dr. Sigmundus]
The Resurrection Fields / by Brian Keaney ; illustrations by Nicoletta Ceccoli. — 1st American ed.
p.   cm. — (Promises of Dr. Sigmundus ; Bk. 3)
"Originally published in Great Britain as The Promises of Dr. Sigmundus: The Mendini Canticle by Orchard Books in 2008"
Summary: Although beset by otherworldly perils, Dante and his best friend Bea continue to be dedicated to the overthrow of Sigmundus and the dark powers that have latched on to his methods of authoritarian mind control.
ISBN 978-0-375-84335-8 (trade) — ISBN 978-0-375-94335-5 (lib. bdg.) —
ISBN 978-0-375-89362-9 (ebook)
[1. Science fiction.] I. Ceccoli, Nicoletta, ill. II. Title.
PZ7.K219Res 2009
[Fic]—dc22
2008041088

ISBN 978-0-440-24012-9 (tr. pbk.)

Printed in the United States of America
March 2011
10 9 8 7 6 5 4 3 2 1

First American Trade Paperback Edition

Between the pedestals of Night and Morning,
Between red death and radiant desire
With not one sound of triumph or of warning
Stands the great sentry on the Bridge of Fire.

James Elroy Flecker, *The Bridge of Fire*

CONTENTS

PROLOGUE

The storm that had raged over the south of Gehenna had finally blown itself out. On a cliff top overlooking a stretch of dark water, a girl in mud-stained clothes stood motionless, a look of shock and terror written across her face. She was staring at two figures a little way off, one lying on the ground, the other crouching nearby. The figure on the ground should have been familiar to every man, woman and child in Gehenna, for he was the leader of their nation. But most people, if they had been told that Dr. Sigmundus was nearby, would have expected to see a much younger man. The pictures of him that hung in official buildings everywhere in the land showed a man in his prime. In truth, however, it had been a very long time since Dr. Sigmundus was in his prime. Only supernatural power had sustained him for all these years, and now, as it drained away from his body, it became clear that he was really very old indeed.

Beside him, Dante Cazabon crouched and waited. He could hardly believe that the struggle was finally over. It had taken so long and cost so much. His friend Ezekiel Semiramis, who had rescued him from the asylum on Tarnagar and taught him about the secret world of the Odyll, was dead. And so was Luther, Dante's brother, whose existence he had not even known about until recently. Indeed, the two of them had only just met, but what should have been a joyful occasion had turned to horror when Luther had tried to kill those who would have been his friends.

Not all of this was Dr. Sigmundus's fault. The dictator had been treacherous, greedy and tyrannical. But he himself had long ago fallen victim to a will far stronger than his own. A being from the depths of the Odyll, a dark current of energy, had possessed him, taking over his mind and body. The name of that being was Orobas, and if his plans had been successful, he would have taken possession of Dante in the same way. It was only the sacrifice of Luther that had defeated him. For rather than kill Dante, Luther had stepped off the edge of the cliff and fallen into the dark waters below.

Dante leaned closer to the body of Dr. Sigmundus. There could be no doubt about it. The old man's eyes were closed and his breathing had stopped. Relieved, Dante let out a long sigh. Then he stood up. He felt no joy at the defeat of his enemy and spat on the ground in disgust.

In that instant Dr. Sigmundus's eyes opened. His thin lips curved upwards in a twisted smile.

"I thank you for your hatred, Dante Cazabon. It was all the invitation I needed."

It was the voice of Orobas. Dr. Sigmundus might be dead, but the creature that possessed his body was still undefeated.

Dante opened his mouth to reply, but instead his whole body shuddered as the creature began to transfer itself to him. He felt his true self shrinking and diminishing. Now he would lose his body and his mind forever. His words faltered. He heard himself screaming. But even as the inarticulate cry of terror tore itself from his lips, in a still place at the center of his mind, he heard his mother's voice. "Remember, Dante," she told him, "it is always now."

Yashar Cazabon had been the first one to uncover the mysteries of the Odyll, and although she had been killed when Dante was only an infant, she had found a way to defy death and come to his aid when he faced his greatest challenges. Now, as she spoke each word with careful emphasis, he suddenly understood what she was trying to tell him. Time could be stretched infinitely. Each moment could be divided again and again without end, and someone who had learned to unite himself with the power of the Odyll could move and act within that extended moment.

He reached into the Odylic realm and immediately sensed the great torrent that was time itself. It surged and boiled around him, like a mighty river, impelled by an endless drive towards the future. He summoned all his strength and held it back. As he did so, he was aware of his enemy's will, angrily responding, determined to overcome his resistance.

He could not hold out against the fury of Orobas forever. They were like two animals that had locked horns, each driving against its opponent with all its might. Sooner or later one of them would weaken. Nor could the river of time be permanently stopped, only paused. He would have to find another way to overthrow his enemy.

Dante searched his mind for the place where he had heard his mother's voice. There it was: the stillness at the center of the hurricane.

"How can I resist him?" he asked.

"You cannot," she replied.

"Then all is lost?" Even as he spoke, he felt the obscene delight of Orobas and knew that his enemy sensed his disappointment.

"You are beaten," Orobas whispered, his words insinuating themselves into Dante's mind like a vile smell.

But his mother spoke again. "Listen to me," she told him. "There is still one course of action open to you. There is a small white bird on a branch of the sycamore tree to your left."

Dante turned and saw the tree she had indicated. It was not yet dawn but there was light enough to make out a bird sitting on a low branch, watching him with its beady eyes.

"Separate your mind from your body," she continued, "and send it forth to take up residence within the body of the bird."

"No!" Orobas hissed. His mind sought to close around Dante's, as though he were catching a fly in his fist.

But Dante was too quick for him. He sent his thought out towards the bird, felt its tiny protest and its bewilderment at finding another being within its body. Then he watched, helpless, as the creature from the depths of the Odyll took possession of the empty body he had left behind.

When the girl on the cliff top heard the scream and saw Dante slump to the ground, she ran towards him, anxious to help. But as she drew nearer, something about the expression on her friend's face made her hesitate. His eyes seemed full of hate.

"Dante?" she said. "Are you all right? It's me, Bea."

Dante got to his feet and lunged clumsily towards her, as though he were unable to control his body properly. Then his hands grasped her by the throat.

"I'm going to kill you," he said, and his voice was as shocking as his words, for it was horribly distorted, as if his tongue had grown too big for his mouth.

Bea struggled furiously to fight him off, but his grip was like iron.

Suddenly a blurred shape appeared between them, and with a cry, Dante released his hold. A bird had appeared from nowhere, pecking at his face savagely, so that he was forced to flail about, trying to drive it away.

Bea did not wait for an explanation of what had just taken place. Sobbing with relief, she turned and fled into the darkness.

COMMANDER BELINSKI'S DILEMMA

Commander Belinski had been security chief of the southwestern region of Gehenna for nearly ten years, but in all that time he had never received an order like this one. He scratched his head and reread the letter, which had arrived by special delivery the night before. It still didn't seem right. With a sigh he summoned his assistant, Gorky, who appeared in the office a moment later, clicking his heels and saluting energetically.

"I want your opinion," Belinski told him.

Gorky nodded. "Certainly, sir."

"This letter arrived yesterday," Belinski continued. "It's from Dr. Sigmundus himself. There's no doubt about its authenticity. I've spoken to the Leader's private secretary by telephone. This is what it says: 'For the attention of Commander Belinski, Thirteenth Southwestern Region. You will meet with your Leader at map reference ST549827 at 0500 hours tomorrow morning, bringing with you a detachment of armed men. You will then transport him without delay to his office in the capital.'" He paused.

"That seems fairly straightforward, sir," Gorky observed.

"Yes," Belinski agreed, "though I've looked up the map reference and it appears to be an abandoned quarry in the middle of nowhere. However, that's not the part that worries me. Listen to what comes next: 'You will not recognize your Leader at first. He will appear to be someone else altogether. But you must not let this stop you from carrying out these orders.' What on earth am I supposed to make of that?"

"It sounds as though Dr. Sigmundus is going to be disguised in some way," Gorky suggested.

"So how the hell am I supposed to recognize him?"

Gorky thought about it. "I expect he'll be the one giving the orders, sir," he said.

Bea returned to the Púca camp and described what had taken place.

"This doesn't make any sense," said Bea's friend Maeve, pushing back her long red hair and frowning. "I spoke to Dante before he left here. He was planning to rescue you."

"Yes, that's what it looked like at first," Bea agreed. "But then he suddenly screamed and collapsed, and when I went over to help him, he grabbed me by the throat and tried to kill me!"

"It must be the shock," Albigen said. One of the Púca's most respected leaders, he was a tall young man with light brown skin, tight curly hair and a jagged scar that ran across his forehead. "Think of all he's had to cope with. I expect he's come to his senses by now. I'll go and talk to him."

"No, wait!" Bea said. She recalled the expression in Dante's eyes as he had lunged towards her. She was certain it would not be as easy as Albigen seemed to think. "I believe something has happened to him, something that has changed his personality."

"What sort of thing?" Albigen asked.

"I don't know. I realize it sounds crazy. But it didn't feel like it really was Dante at all. It felt like he'd been taken over."

Albigen looked skeptical.

"He was Dante when he left here," Maeve pointed out.

"Yes, but something very strange happened on the cliff top,"

Bea said. "I can't explain it, but I don't think Albigen should just walk right up to him."

"I'll be careful," Albigen told her.

"She's hysterical," he said to himself as he walked away. No doubt Dante was also hysterical. It was understandable. The world had been turned upside down for all of them in the last few hours, and shock did strange things to people. When he had lived in the north amid the Ichor mines, he had seen a woman burst out laughing when she was told that her husband had been killed in an accident underground. She hadn't known what she was doing, and Dante was probably in the same state. The important thing was to keep a cool head. He would approach Dante carefully, talk to him gently and remind him that they were friends. Then he would bring him back to the Púca and all would be well.

It was easy enough to follow the trail of footprints left behind in the mud, and it didn't take long to find the place where Luther and Bea had left the cover of the trees for the cliff top. Albigen paused and squinted into the distance. Yes, he could see Dante standing outlined against the sky. Albigen hesitated. It was important to remember that, whereas he had only his powers of persuasion and his own strength, Dante had the power of the Odyll at his disposal.

He could just about make out a body lying on the ground beside Dante. So it must be true, as Bea had claimed, that Dr. Sigmundus was dead. If so, then the struggle was really over. But Albigen was not ready to accept that yet. At least, not without proof. He had been fighting Dr. Sigmundus for too long to be easily taken in.

Cautiously, he prepared to step out from among the trees, but before he could do so, he heard the sound of an engine in the distance. He froze and listened. There must be a road on the other side of the cliff, hidden by the rising ground. Soon the sound grew louder, and it was clear that more than one vehicle was making determined progress towards this location. Suddenly, three trucks appeared on the horizon. Keeping under cover of the trees, Albigen drew nearer until he was close enough to see and hear what was happening.

The trucks came to a halt. Security officers jumped out and immediately surrounded Dante, their weapons pointing directly at him. The commanding officer glanced at the body of Dr. Sigmundus and then at Dante. "Don't move an inch!" he barked. "Tell me what has happened to the Leader."

Dante stared calmly back at him. "*I* am your Leader," he replied.

The commander frowned. "Shoot him if he moves," he ordered his men. Then he stepped towards the body of Dr. Sigmundus and crouched down beside it.

"*I* am your Leader," Dante repeated. His voice was cold and hard, and despite the fact that more than a dozen rifles were being pointed at him, he managed to sound incredibly threatening. "You have had your orders, Commander Belinski," he continued. "You are to take me to the capital without delay. We can bring this body with us, since you seem so concerned with its welfare. But let us waste no more time here."

The commander stood up. His face was only inches from Dante's now. "Are you completely insane?" he shouted. "You are under arrest for the murder of Dr. Sigmundus."

He turned his head slightly to give an order to his men, and in that instant Dante grabbed him by the throat. Then two things happened simultaneously. The world appeared to ripple. That was the only way Albigen could describe it. At the same time he heard the sound of rifles firing, and the commander fell to the ground.

Intellectually Albigen knew what had happened. Dante had used Odylic Force to change reality. But emotionally it was still hard for him to accept. He stared at the scene in confusion. The soldiers, too, looked utterly bewildered. Only Dante remained unperturbed.

"Who is next in command?" Dante asked.

One of the security guards stepped nervously forward. "I am."

"And your name is?"

"Assistant Commander Gorky."

"Very well, Assistant Commander Gorky. Listen carefully, and let's hope that you are not a fool, like your ex-colleague here. Your men will not be able to kill me. If you order them to try again, they will kill you instead. Is that perfectly clear?"

Gorky nodded slowly.

"Good. Now, it may seem to you that the world has come to an end. But that is most assuredly not the case. Yes, your Leader is dead, but I am his successor in every way. The country will be secure in my hands because I am the new Dr. Sigmundus. Is that clear?"

"Yes, sir."

"Good. Now, are you ready to take me to Ellison?"

Assistant Commander Gorky's heels snapped together and he saluted crisply.

Albigen watched with fear and confusion as Dante and Gorky got into the lead truck while the other security guards lifted the body of Dr. Sigmundus into an accompanying vehicle. Had Dante really chosen to follow in the footsteps of their enemy, or was he playing some elaborate and deadly game?

When the vehicles had disappeared over the brow of the hill, Albigen rose from his hiding place and walked slowly back through the trees, trying to decide what he would say to the others.

* * *

From its perch on the sycamore tree, a little bird observed the scene. Behind its eyes, Dante—the real Dante—watched with a profound sense of gloom. His former body had become a mindless puppet, with Orobas pulling its strings. He wanted to cry out in anger and frustration, but all he could do was force a tiny note of protest out of the creature's beak.

"Do not despair," his mother's voice promised. "I will help you."

The bird spread its wings and took to the air.

OSMAN

Nyro Balash knew he ought to forget his friend Luther, but in practice he simply couldn't do it. The arguments for putting Luther out of his mind were both powerful and convincing. First there was the fact that Luther had got him into the worst trouble he'd ever faced. This had happened when the two of them were hiking in the wilderness that lay between Tavor, where they lived, and Gehenna, the closed country to the south.

During this hike the two boys had stumbled upon a field of exotic purple flowers surrounded by a wire fence. Those flowers, which had looked so beautiful, had nearly proved deadly to Luther. He had experienced some sort of seizure when he tried to smell them. If soldiers had not turned up with an antidote, he might not have survived. But the arrival of those soldiers was no coincidence. It turned out that Nyro and Luther were trespassing on government property. They were arrested and interrogated for hours. When they were finally allowed to return home, it was made very clear that if they even whispered about what had happened, both they and their parents would be charged under the State Secrets Act.

Nyro's parents, frightened out of their wits, had warned him firmly to stay away from Luther in the future. But if that had been the only consequence of their mountain hike, things might not have been so bad. His parents couldn't keep tabs on him all the time. Eventually, when all the fuss had died down, the two boys could have quietly resumed their friendship. But from the time he got back from the mountains, Luther began acting increasingly strange. He became silent and withdrawn. And the few words he did say—they didn't make any sense. He took to sleeping outside in the yard, and one night Nyro secretly followed him to Liminal Park, a stretch of open land on the outskirts of town, and watched as Luther stood on a hilltop, howling at the moon. On another occasion he had looked on in dismay as his friend caught a fly in his hand, put it in his mouth and *ate* it!

Then one day Nyro had been in the middle of a conversation with Luther—admittedly a fairly one-sided conversation since his friend just kept staring into space while Nyro tried repeatedly to get through to him—when, suddenly, Luther jumped to his feet and ran out of the room. No one had seen him since.

No sooner had Luther vanished than everybody started acting as if he had never existed in the first place. Teachers and classmates, boys he had played football with every Saturday, all looked puzzled whenever Nyro mentioned Luther's name and shook their heads in confusion. "I don't recall anyone of that name," they insisted. The school secretary even assured him that there had never been a Luther Vavohu enrolled at their school.

Nyro had no idea what it all meant, but he was determined to find out, even if it meant getting in trouble with the authorities again. Luther had been a good friend, and Nyro wasn't about to give up on him just because somebody in a uniform didn't want him to know what was going on. He decided to start by talking to Luther's mother.

And so he found himself making his way this evening along Luther's street, arriving just in time to see two military vehicles pulling up outside of his friend's house. One was a jeep, the other a large truck. Fortunately, Nyro was still on the opposite side of the street. He ducked into a yard and crouched down behind the hedge, watching as a familiar figure stepped out of the first vehicle. It was Brigadier Giddings, the man who had interrogated him and

Luther. Followed by two armed soldiers, the Brigadier walked up to the front door of Luther's house and rang the bell.

Luther's mother appeared, and there was a brief conversation between the two of them. Nyro had the impression that an argument of some kind was taking place. Finally she was led away. Nyro watched as she climbed into the back of the truck, which then drove off at high speed.

Now more soldiers got out of the second vehicle and made their way inside the house. Soon they began to re-emerge, carrying boxes. Some of them clutched items of furniture, all of which they stowed carefully in the back of the truck.

"What exactly are you doing?"

Nyro turned around to see a very tall, very thin man standing beside him. He had a great mane of white hair, and there was something distinctly old-fashioned about his clothes, as if he had stepped out of another time. This was probably the owner of the yard in which he was squatting.

"I was just trying to see what was happening on the other side of the street," Nyro said, without moving from his hiding place.

"I gathered that," the white-haired gentleman observed. "But I couldn't help wondering why you felt it was necessary to do so from behind my hedge."

Nyro considered this question. It was hard to know what to say in reply. Finally he decided he might as well tell the truth.

"I'm not supposed to have anything to do with the people who live in that house," he admitted. "If the soldiers see me, I'll be in big trouble."

"How interesting!" the white-haired gentleman said. He studied Nyro more carefully, as if he were a collector of insects examining a particularly fascinating specimen. "Perhaps you'd better come inside and tell me a bit more," he said at last.

"Well, I'm not . . . ," Nyro began.

But the white-haired gentleman interrupted him. "Of course, I could just attract the attention of our military friends over there."

"All right, I'm coming."

"Splendid!" The white-haired gentleman clasped his hands together in satisfaction.

The inside of the house, like the gentleman's clothes, suggested that it belonged to an earlier period. Through an open door Nyro glimpsed a sitting room full of dark oak furniture. His companion led the way to a book-lined study at the very top of the house. In one corner of the room a large wooden desk, piled high with papers, stood opposite a rather battered-looking leather armchair.

"Do sit down," the white-haired gentleman said.

Nyro perched uneasily on the armchair.

"We should introduce ourselves," his host continued, sitting down at the desk. "My name is Osman. And you are?"

"Nyro."

"Very good, Nyro. You know, I have a strong feeling about you. When I saw you crouched down behind my hedge, it was almost as if you were set apart from your surroundings, as if you had been touched by something from another world. Does that make any sense to you?"

Nyro shook his head. "No. I mean yes. I mean I don't know. Some very odd things have been happening to me lately."

Osman smiled, showing a set of teeth that any horse would have been proud to own. "Wonderful! I do like to hear about odd things. Would you care for some tea while you tell me all about them?"

"I don't really like tea, thanks."

Osman looked astonished. "Not like tea! Well, all I can say is you miss a great deal. However, I am certainly going to have some. I can't get through the evening without a good, strong cup of tea."

14

He pressed a button on the wall and Nyro heard a bell ring deep in the bowels of the house.

"Now then, my young friend, start at the beginning, don't leave anything out and don't stop until you get all the way to my hedge."

Though he had only agreed to tell his story under threat of being exposed to Brigadier Giddings, Nyro found it quite a relief to get the whole thing off his chest. Osman listened, only interrupting from time to time to clarify some of the details. Halfway through, they were interrupted by the arrival of an ancient butler carrying a tray on which was placed a quite enormous cup and saucer. He set it down on the desk without so much as a glance in Nyro's direction.

"So," Osman continued, after the butler had left, "you were just telling me about how everyone seemed to have forgotten all about your friend Luther."

Nyro nodded. "His mother's been taken away and he doesn't even seem to be on the school records anymore. There's practically no proof that he ever existed. Except for this."

He reached into his inside pocket and took out a photograph of himself and Luther. It had been taken a few days before they had set off on their hiking trip. He handed it to Osman, who started visibly as he glanced at it.

"I've met this young man," he announced.

"What do you mean?"

"Exactly what I say. I have already made the acquaintance of your friend."

"How?"

"He came to a lecture I gave a couple of months ago."

Nyro shook his head. "I think you must be mistaken. Luther wouldn't do something like that. He was always cutting classes at school."

"I have a very good memory for faces," Osman insisted. "Besides, your friend came up to me afterwards. He said he had a number of questions he wanted to ask me."

"What was this lecture about, then?" Nyro asked.

"Poetry," Osman told him.

"Listen, I can guarantee you that Luther would not have gone to a talk about poetry," Nyro said with a certain amount of scorn.

Osman gave him a long, hard look, and the smile faded from Nyro's face. There was something about the old man's eyes that forced you to respect him, a kind of power that seemed to radiate from deep inside him. "It seems that you are not quite as intelligent as your friend," he said.

Nyro opened his mouth to reply, but Osman cut him off. "Have you ever heard of the Mendini Canticle?" he asked.

"No."

"It's a lost work written by the Gehennan poet Alvar Kazimir Mendini. Mendini was a rather special individual. Some people claim that his poem predicts the end of the world. Unfortunately, he was assassinated by agents of the Gehennan government before he could publish it."

"Why?"

"Because Mendini was a member of the Púca, a group of people who were seeking to overthrow the leadership of Dr. Sigmundus."

"Was that what your lecture was about?"

"Yes. Your friend told me he was interested in everything to do with Gehenna, and especially with Mendini."

"Amazing," Nyro remarked.

"You said you went hiking in the border area before he disappeared. Whose idea was that?" Osman asked.

"Luther's."

Osman raised one eyebrow in a gesture that seemed to say, "You see? Not so amazing, really."

"All right, but that still doesn't explain where he's gone and why everyone seems to be forgetting about him."

Osman nodded. "True. This reminds me of something I read about once." He got up and went over to the window. "Our military friends seem to have gone away, for the time being at least. What do you say we go and take a look inside your friend's house?"

"How will we get in if his mother's not there?"

"We will simply break in, of course," Osman said. He rubbed his hands together and smiled gleefully. "Let me see now." He opened a cupboard and began ransacking its contents. "No need for subtlety, I shouldn't think." He took out a small hammer from the cupboard and put it in his pocket. "Now then, what about the guard dog, eh?"

Nyro frowned. "I don't think there's a dog," he said.

Osman merely smiled and handed him an oblong mirror in a carved wooden frame. It was about the size of a large book. "You can look after this for me," he said. "But keep it wrapped up until I tell you. That's *very* important." He passed Nyro a black velvet cloth. "Don't leave any of the glass showing, please. We wouldn't want to annoy anyone until the time is right."

Nyro wrapped the mirror in the black velvet cloth. He was beginning to wonder whether the old man was not right in the head.

Osman's face positively beamed with expectation. "Splendid!" he said. "Now then, let's get on with the job."

Luther's house backed onto an unlit alley. It was a simple matter to get up onto a trash can and climb over the back wall without being seen. Osman showed surprising agility for a man of his years.

Once they were over the wall, Osman took the hammer out of his pocket and smashed a pane of glass. It made a lot of noise, and Nyro expected the neighbors to pop their heads out of their windows at any moment, though Osman seemed entirely unperturbed. He reached through the open window and opened the back door.

"We'd better go through the house systematically," Osman said. "We'll start downstairs and work our way up." He peered around the kitchen, opening cupboards and drawers.

"What are we looking for?" Nyro asked.

"I'll tell you when I find it," Osman replied.

Nyro and Osman made their way through the dining room and the living room. The soldiers had done a comprehensive job. Practically everything that could be easily moved had been taken from the house. There were broken ornaments, pictures had been removed from the walls and thrown onto the floor, and the sofa had been slit open. What were they looking for?

Upstairs Luther's bedroom had been stripped almost completely bare. Even the mattress had been taken off the bed. The doors of his wardrobe hung open a little forlornly. Osman stood in the middle of the room, his nose twitching slightly, like a dog's when it catches a new scent.

"I've got a feeling about this room," he said.

"Like the one you had about me?" Nyro asked.

Osman shook his head. "That was a good feeling," he replied. "I wonder if—" But he broke off. Someone was opening the front door. "In here, quick!" he whispered urgently.

They both stepped into the wardrobe and Osman closed the doors behind them. A moment later Nyro heard footsteps coming up the stairs. He held his breath and peered through the crack between the doors as Brigadier Giddings came into the room, carrying something in both hands. He set it down carefully in the middle of the floor, then turned and went back downstairs. They heard the front door close once more. Nyro breathed a sigh of relief.

Nyro and Osman emerged from the wardrobe and crossed the room to examine the object that the Brigadier had placed on the floor. It was a bowl filled with a dark red liquid.

Osman picked the bowl up and sniffed its contents. He shook his head. "This is very bad news indeed," he said.

"Why? What is it?" Nyro asked.

Osman put the bowl back down in the middle of the floor. "It's blood," he said. "And it's extremely fresh."

KIDU

"Giddim!"

It took Dante several days to realize that it wasn't just a noise. The bird was actually talking.

"Giddim! Aaach, aaach, aaach giddim!"

At least that was what it sounded like. But it had to mean something. Dante could tell, because he shared the bird's mind. There was intention behind its cries. A desire to communicate.

Most of the time he tried to ignore the bird's thoughts—if you could actually call them thoughts. A lot of them were simply grumbles about itching under its feathers or the difficulty of finding enough bugs to eat. He tried to shut himself off in the way that you shut yourself off from the conversations going on all around you when you stand in the middle of a crowd. He had enough on his own mind to keep him busy—if only he had got to the Púca's campsite more quickly; if only he hadn't underestimated Orobas; if only he hadn't allowed himself to be overtaken by rage; if only he hadn't turned his back. If only, if only, if only . . .

"Giddim! Aaach, aaach, aaach giddim!"

He was becoming increasingly certain that the bird's comments weren't just general expressions of feeling, like making a claim to the territory around it, complaining about the cold or the lack of food. It was addressing itself directly to him.

"Giddim!"

Trapped inside the bird's body, with no solution on the horizon, Dante found that the repetitive cry was starting to get him down.

"Giddim!"

"All right!" Dante said wearily. "All right! I've heard you. 'Giddim.' But what's it supposed to mean?"

"You."

Had he just imagined that, or had the bird really replied? No! Of course not. He was letting himself get carried away. It was understandable. He longed so much to talk to someone, to discuss his predicament, that his mind had begun playing tricks on him.

"*You* are Giddim!"

There it was again! He really could understand what the bird was saying. After all, they shared the same brain. Perhaps if he just tried to feel the meaning behind the sounds instead of expecting the bird to speak in his own language . . .

"Why do you call me Giddim?" he demanded.

"It is what you are—a thing that has no body of its own! Leave me!" the bird demanded. "You have no right to live inside me!"

So a giddim was a creature that took possession of another being's body. A parasite, like Orobas.

That was how it began. Over the next few days he learned more about the bird. His name was Kidu. And he hated Dante for forcing him to do things in which he had no interest whatsoever. Like attacking Dante's former body when Orobas had tried to use it to kill Bea. But most of all Kidu hated Dante for being inside him. Dante tried explaining that he had no wish to share Kidu's body, but the bird wouldn't listen. He was too busy being mad at him— and worrying.

Surprisingly, Kidu wasn't just worried about Dante. There was something even bigger. Something that he called Shurruppak, and whatever this Shurruppak was, it was getting worse all the time.

"Shurruppak growing. Soon Shurruppak cover all. Swallow all. Everything become Shurruppak. Kidu gone. All zimbir gone. Nothing. End."

Kidu repeated this little formula to himself over and over again while he perched on a branch, occasionally pecking at the tiny insects that lived beneath the bark of the tree. Dante racked his brains to decide what it could mean.

Two other birds landed on a branch above Kidu. Once they would have been indistinguishable to Dante, but now that he saw them through Kidu's eyes, he had no difficulty recognizing them as distinct individuals. Kidu said something to the larger of the two, but it made no reply. Then the two birds flew rapidly away.

Kidu flapped his wings in what Dante now recognized as a gesture of anger. "Shurruppak bring Giddim. Filthy Giddim. Zimbir dislike Kidu now. No talk anymore."

"Was that Zimbir you spoke to just now?" Dante asked.

Kidu directed a wave of contempt at him. "Stupid Giddim. All zimbir. All."

Suddenly Dante understood. "Zimbir" was not the name of the bird that had just flown away. All birds were zimbir, and they all disliked Kidu because of the giddim that possessed him.

"I'm sorry," Dante said.

"Kidu don't need sorry. Go back to Shurruppak!"

"What is Shurruppak?"

An explosion of rage filled Kidu's mind. "You know Shurruppak!" he told him. "You belong Shurruppak!"

"I don't know. Why don't you show it to me?"

"No!"

"You want me to leave, don't you?"

As soon as he said this, Kidu's attitude changed. Dante could feel the bird concentrating every fiber of his being on him. "I show you Shurruppak, you leave?" Kidu demanded eagerly.

"I will try," Dante promised. "I cannot guarantee, but if it is possible, then I will leave."

Kidu hesitated. "No tricks?" he said.

"No tricks."

"I show you Shurruppak!" Kidu spread his wings and took to the sky.

Before Kidu had only made short flights from one tree to another. But now, as he flew high in the sky, there was a grace and a joyfulness about the flight that was exhilarating. Kidu's wings rose and fell steadily, as if he were rowing through the air, negotiating wind currents with delicate movements of his wing tips and tail feathers. It was clear to Dante that flying was more than just a means for Kidu to get from one place to another. It was a part of the bird's identity, a way of demonstrating his place in the world.

"Annalugu," Kidu told him. He had obviously been listening in on Dante's thoughts. From the tone in which he said this, Dante felt certain it was not meant as an insult, like "Giddim" had been.

"Not you," Kidu said impatiently. "This is annalugu. The paths of the air that belong to the zimbir and no one else. Where the thousand journeys are made."

"The thousand journeys?"

"You know nothing, Giddim," Kidu replied scornfully. "The thousand journeys come before the one journey when every zimbir must leave annalugu for the Hidden Path that lies on the other side of the air in the Sky Beyond the Sky." Kidu spoke these words solemnly and Dante could feel the importance that he attached to this Hidden Path. But then the bird's mood seemed to change completely. "Perhaps Kidu will not find the Hidden Path when his time comes," he said, and his words were filled with sadness.

"Why not?"

"Shurruppak destroy Hidden Path!" Kidu declared angrily. After that he remained silent no matter how many questions Dante tried to ask.

It was a long journey, and Dante soon lost track of their direction. Dante could only guess how Kidu knew where he was going, but he sensed the bird's certainty as Kidu navigated the paths of the air—or annalugu, as Kidu called them—while the sun dropped lower in the sky and the Forgill Mountains came into sight.

Dante had crossed these mountains with his friend Malachy Mazotta. Malachy had been the supervisor of the cemetery where Dante had hidden after fleeing from the clutches of Dr. Sigmundus. Instead of handing Dante over to the authorities, Malachy had joined him, and the two of them had hijacked a plane and made their escape. In search of the Púca's camp, they had been forced to land on the other side of these mountains, in a place where the everyday world and the Odylic realm were so mixed up that Dante had felt Odylic Force clinging to him like fog from the moment he had stepped down from the plane. Was that where Kidu was headed?

"Shurruppak soon!" the bird assured him.

The mountain range was directly below them now, and Dante caught a sudden glimpse of vivid purple. He recalled seeing exactly the same thing when he and Malachy had flown low over these mountain peaks, searching desperately for somewhere to land. Abruptly the steady beat of Kidu's wings ceased, and he began a series of circular, gliding maneuvers.

"Close enough," he announced.

"But what is it?" Dante demanded.

Kidu gave an incredulous squawk. "Giddim use Kidu's eyes!" he ordered angrily. "Giddim not talk. Giddim look."

Dante had already found that he could see the world as he had been accustomed to seeing it through human eyes, but if he concentrated very hard, he could also see the world the way that Kidu looked at it. That was what he tried to do now.

Immediately the landscape below him came into much sharper focus. The purple blur became a field of purple flowers, each one swaying gently in the breeze. Around the field was a chain-link fence. A soldier in camouflage uniform was driving around its perimeter in an open-topped jeep. The dirt road on which he was traveling led away from the field, through scrubland to the military base where Dante and Malachy had been held prisoner. Beside the military base was the landing strip on which they had brought down their plane.

Hovering over the field was a circle of darkness. It was not particularly large, no more than a couple of yards in diameter, but it was utterly black, as if in that spot even the possibility of light had been extinguished.

"What is that?" Dante asked.

"Shurruppak."

"What does it do?"

"It eats."

"What does it eat?"

"*Everything*. At first it only tiny. Like speck of dust. But muzur notice. Fly too close. Whoosh! Gone. Shurruppak get bigger. Zimbir notice. Curious. Some zimbir fly too close. Whoosh! Zimbir gone. Shurruppak bigger still."

Dante thought about this. He guessed that muzur were probably insects, and of course zimbir were birds. So whatever else this circle of blackness did, it swallowed up any creature that got too close.

Suddenly Kidu grew tense. "Watch!" he ordered. "Shurruppak getting ready."

Sure enough, some sort of change was taking place at the

center of the circle. It began to ripple and then to seethe, almost like water that was coming to the boil. Suddenly a finger of darkness shot downwards from its center towards the field. It was like a bolt of dark lightning. A moment later the finger of darkness was gone, and with it, the soldier and his jeep.

"See!" Kidu declared triumphantly. "Silly zittenziteen go about field all day in stink-move-noise-thing. Careless. Busy guarding field. Not look up. Whoosh! Gone."

"What happened to him?" Dante asked.

"You know what happened to him!" Kidu declared angrily. "You belong Shurruppak."

"Why do you say that?" Dante asked.

"All zimbir know story of beginning."

"I don't know it. Tell me the story."

"No. Giddim go now. Go back to Shurruppak."

"I can't, Kidu. I'm sorry."

"You promised!"

"I can't leave until I get my body back. I *don't* belong to Shurruppak, whatever you think, but I think I know who is behind it. Maybe if you tell me your story . . . ?"

"Kidu not tell story! Giddim liar!"

Suddenly Kidu's mood changed. He pulled out of his slow circular glide and began flying rapidly away.

Dante sensed the bird's panic. "What is it?" he asked.

"Huwawa!" Kidu turned his head upwards and Dante caught a glimpse of a much larger bird, descending rapidly towards them from a great height. It looked like some kind of hawk.

Dante could tell that Kidu was putting all his strength into trying to escape, but his small wings were no match for those of the bigger bird. In almost no time it was directly above. A moment later Dante felt a searing pain as the bird's talons raked across Kidu's neck. Dante felt Kidu's pain and his waning strength.

Desperately he sought to find a connection to the Odylic realm. Ezekiel Semiramis had taught him, "Along with our physical body, each of us possesses another body that dwells within us, invisible and unknown. Let us call it the phantom. This phantom is made of the same stuff as the Odyll and always wants to return to its source. Discover the phantom within yourself and you will find the gateway to the Odyll."

Dante's phantom now shared Kidu's physical body. So the gateway to the Odylic realm must still be within Dante's reach. "Stop worrying about your physical body," he told himself. "Summon the gateway."

But before he could even begin to compose himself for the act of will that this involved, the hawk plunged once more, and its talons raked Kidu's back. With a cry of pain Kidu began falling helplessly towards the ground. "Don't give up!" Dante urged, but there was no response.

As Kidu was hurtling downwards with increasing speed, Dante struggled to visualize the gray door that would open into that other world of which this one was a mere shadow.

The door took shape in his mind, and immediately the power of the Odyll flowed out towards him. "You are not falling," he told Kidu. "There is nowhere to fall, nowhere except everywhere."

He felt the bird's confusion as Kidu opened his eyes and found that everything had changed. To Dante's surprise, however, the world of the Odyll appeared different to him now that he was seeing it through Kidu's eyes. Before him stretched an endless plain of blue, gray and violet, across which great masses of creamy clouds drifted, traversed by a zigzagged trail that seemed to be made of millions of golden and silver sparks. "The Hidden Path!" Kidu said, his voice filled with awe. "Then Kidu is . . ."

"No," Dante told him. "You are not dead."

"Kidu not survive fall. Not possible."

"You did not hit the ground," Dante told him. "I took us away."

"How?"

"I am a giddim," Dante said, with a touch of irony. "But we cannot stay here," he continued. "I don't have enough power to hold us here. Besides, it is not yet time for you to take the Hidden Path."

Dante forced himself to ignore what Kidu was seeing and to use his own vision instead. Immediately he found himself surrounded by the ever-changing forms of the Odyll. They rushed past him, borne on the great current of time. But he knew that, like Kidu's Hidden Path, this procession of images was only an illusion. Beyond it was another, deeper level where the power of the Odyll was unrestrained, and it was into this ocean of formless energy that Dante now reached. Instantly he was filled with such strength that he felt like a match that flares up brilliantly, only to be burned away into lifeless ash. He struggled to keep himself separate—to be filled with power but not utterly consumed.

Just as he felt certain that the power was his to command, he became aware of another consciousness, one that was all too horribly familiar. Orobas had been alerted to his presence in the Odylic world, and now he began to turn all the force of his attention in Dante's direction. In a moment Dante would be fully in his sight, and then Dante would face a battle for the survival of his self, a battle he was far from sure that he could win. He knew he must retreat, remember the world he had left behind, imagine himself within the body of Kidu, perched on a branch somewhere safe, and order his phantom to take them both there. This picture began to form itself in his mind. At the same time he sensed a glowing form beside him, and for the briefest of instants, his mother's voice whispered in his ear.

"On Enil's Tower there is a message for Bea."

Then he and Kidu were once more in the everyday world.

"The Hidden Path!" Kidu said mournfully. "You show Kidu, then make him come back here. Not fair. Kidu hurting. Let him finish the thousand journeys now, go back and take the Hidden Path."

"I'm sorry, Kidu, but you will return, I promise you."

Kidu said nothing for a long time, and Dante sensed that the bird was deep in thought. Finally he spoke. "Kidu rest. Get well. Tell story of beginning. Then Giddim understand everything."

"Thank you, Kidu."

"Kidu thank Giddim."

THE BEEHIVE HUTS

Urged on by Albigen's description of what he had seen, the Púca packed quickly and left their camp. Many struggled to accept that Dante had switched sides. Nevertheless, the presence of a detachment of armed security guards on the nearby cliff top was a fact that could not be ignored.

It was impossible for more than a hundred people to travel across the country in a line of trucks and cars without drawing some attention to themselves. But fortunately, this part of Gehenna had been largely depopulated when the majority of the inhabitants had been forced north to work in the Ichor mines. So the Púca's exodus passed largely unnoticed, though here and there a bewildered farmhand stood in a field, gaping at the convoy of ramshackle vehicles that rattled past.

Bea sat beside Albigen, expecting to be set upon by security guards at any moment, but her fears proved groundless. "Perhaps our enemies have already set off for Ellison?" she thought, then shook her head in confusion. Even though it was less than an hour since Dante had tried to kill her, it was difficult to think of him as her enemy. What would his next move be? she wondered.

In a heavily wooded area Albigen turned off the road onto an old logging track. No vehicles had been this way for a long time, and the trail was quite overgrown in places. Eventually it petered out altogether, and Albigen stopped his truck. One by one the others came to a halt in a semicircle behind him. This was where they would lay Ezekiel to rest.

It was Manachee, Maeve's father and Ezekiel's longtime friend, who dug the grave. Tree roots held the earth in an iron grip but Manachee refused to be deterred. Muscles straining, his face smudged with dirt and sweat, he drove his spade into the ground repeatedly until the hole grew so deep that he was forced to stand within it and shovel the earth upwards. At last it was deep enough. Then he and Albigen lowered Ezekiel's body, wrapped in a white cotton sheet, gently into the grave.

Everyone stood in mute respect, overcome by their sadness. Then Maeve spoke. "Before we met Ezekiel, we were afraid to speak of our dreams, afraid to own up to who we really are. We knew we were different but did not dare admit it," she reminded them. "He helped us conquer that fear and showed us we are not alone. He taught us how to stand up and fight. We will not give up now that he is no longer with us. We will carry on the struggle and make him proud of us." With this, they shoveled the earth back into the grave and marked the spot with a little pile of stones.

Afterwards they discussed where they ought to head next. "About half a day's journey to the east of here is what used to be one of the most famous sites in Gehenna," Manachee told them. "Nobody bothers about it now because people have forgotten their history, but Alvar took me there once. He used to go there quite often to seek inspiration."

Bea recalled that Manachee had also been friends with Dante's father, Alvar Mendini, the famous poet.

"It's a mysterious stone pillar built on a hilltop with a collection of cone-shaped buildings beside it," Manachee went on. "Alvar used to say they looked like giant beehives. Nobody knows much about the people who built them, except that they lived over a thousand years ago. But it's a good spot because you can see for miles in all directions. It would be difficult for anyone to sneak up on us."

Glad to have a destination and a plan, the Púca got back into their vehicles and continued on their way, picking roads that were seldom used. By late afternoon they had reached the hill on which the ancient monument had been built. Here the road narrowed considerably, snaking around the hillside alarmingly with a sheer drop on one side. The engine of the truck in which Bea sat whined in protest as the ascent grew ever steeper. Albigen's face was a mask of concentration, and he gripped the steering wheel so hard that his knuckles turned white.

At last they reached the top, and there it was: a stone pillar about three times the height of a man, with a set of steps spiraling around it and a platform at the top just large enough for someone to stand on.

The huts beside it had been made from individual stones placed carefully, one on top of the other, in ever-decreasing circles. They seemed as ancient as the land on which they stood. Each one was large enough for three or four people to share, though there would not be much privacy. Manachee had been quite correct. It was a wonderful spot for a camp. North, south and west you could see for miles. To the east reared Mount Sulyaman, the country's tallest mountain.

But Bea felt puzzled by the pillar. With such an unimpeded view of the countryside all around, why had the ancient people felt the need to build a lookout post?

"Nobody really knows," Manachee told her. "Perhaps it was just a monument."

"Then why the steps and the platform at the top?" she wondered.

Bea and Maeve elected to share a hut. They were carrying their belongings from the trucks when Bea noticed a bright green lizard clinging to the outside of their hut. On its back was a distinctive marking almost in the shape of a key. As she watched, the lizard's dark tongue flicked in and out in search of insects. A moment later the lizard disappeared into a crack between two stones.

Manachee passed by and saw what she was looking at. "They're a feature of this place," he told her. "There's even a picture of one on the wall of the meetinghouse."

The meetinghouse was a larger, square building set apart from the others. After she had finished unpacking, Bea decided to take a look at it. The building was constructed of regular stone blocks. It must once have possessed a timber roof, though that had long since rotted away. Despite being exposed to the elements, the mural that Manachee had described was remarkably well preserved, its colors and details still bright and clear. It showed an enormous man lying on the hillside. Compared to him, the huts were no bigger than thimbles. In the foreground of the picture was one of the lizards Bea had seen earlier. Next to the lizard was a bell.

Manachee came into the meetinghouse while she was studying the mural. "It's known as the Sleeping Giant," he told her.

"What does it represent?"

"Oh, there have been all sorts of theories. Some historians have suggested that the ancient people of Gehenna believed this world was no more than the dream of a sleeping giant and that it would end when he woke up. But the study of our history was discouraged after Dr. Sigmundus came to power, so we don't really know anything beyond speculation."

"But what do *you* think it means?" Bea asked.

Manachee raised one eyebrow. "Well, I like to think that bell in the foreground is a symbol of hope, somehow."

After a while the rest of the Púca gathered in the meeting-house to admire the mural and make plans. Food was high on the agenda. They had enough to feed themselves for the time being but would need to increase their supplies before too long. Bea and Seersha volunteered to drive to the nearest town the following morning to see what it had to offer. There might be a government warehouse that could be raided. Failing that, since the Púca still possessed a small stock of money left over from previous raids, they could at least buy a few staples like flour and rice.

The next morning they set off for the town of Podmyn dressed in the overalls of farmworkers. They parked on the outskirts and made their way towards the center as casually as they could. It was clear from the faded grandeur of many of the buildings that Podmyn had once been a thriving town. The covered market in the town square stood opposite the pillared entrance to an imposing red-brick building that bore the name of Podmyn District Corn Exchange. But its windows were boarded up now, as were those of many of the adjoining shops. In recent years the movement of local people to the Ichor mines in the north of the country had brought leaner times. A little knot of elderly men sat at wooden tables outside a grubby-looking café, eyeing the strangers suspiciously. Seersha gave them a nod as she walked past but got no response.

"Friendly bunch!" Seersha said under her breath to Bea.

"Look at this," Bea told her, pointing to a notice in the window of a grocer's shop. " 'A special television broadcast will take place at 11 a.m. on Monday,' " she read. " 'It is required viewing for all citizens.' "

Very few people in Gehenna could afford their own televisions. There was one in each Dagabo, the meeting place where people gathered every week to take Ichor. In addition some shops and offices had them.

Seersha glanced at the clock on the top of the corn exchange, which still seemed to be working despite the abandoned building that it now graced. "That's in five minutes' time," she observed.

"Should we go inside?" Bea asked.

The shopkeeper was a small, pasty-faced man. Bea noticed that he wore a built-up shoe since one of his legs was shorter than the other—the likely reason he had not been conscripted to work in the Ichor mines.

"The television's in the back room," he told them, pointing to a curtained doorway.

Rows of wooden chairs had been set out in front of the television set in the inner room. A group of elderly women had already claimed the first two rows. Bea and Seersha took seats in the back.

The room quickly filled up, but the audience sat in silence, their eyes trained on the blank screen. At last the shopkeeper limped into the room and turned on the television. Military music began to play over a picture of the flag of Gehenna. Then a news broadcaster appeared on the screen. "My fellow citizens," he began, "it is with the greatest sorrow that I must inform you of the death of our beloved Leader, Dr. Sigmundus."

Most of the audience looked utterly shocked at these words, and many cried out in dismay. The broadcaster went on to describe how their leader had passed away peacefully in his sleep, and how members of the government, top civil servants and security chiefs had paid tribute to his work in developing Ichor, the miracle drug that had rescued the country from barbarism by changing people's behavior, and in doing so had created the modern, healthy society from which they all benefited. He told them that special buses would be available for all those who wanted to witness the funeral. It would take place in two days' time in Ellison, the capital city.

"There is some comfort for the people of Gehenna in this, their darkest hour," the broadcaster continued. "A successor has already been appointed. And in order to ensure continuity of leadership, the swearing-in ceremony will take place on the same day as the funeral. The face of our Leader-Designate will be unfamiliar to most of you. However, you can rest assured that he was chosen for the position by Dr. Sigmundus himself. This is the first official picture of our future Leader."

As a photograph of a smiling Dante appeared on the screen, Bea and Seersha looked at each other in horror.

"Leading figures in the government have welcomed the appointment, and the Leader-Designate has graciously accepted their pledges of loyalty. In his first statement, issued this morning, he has promised to continue the work of his illustrious predecessor and announced that henceforth he will be known as Sigmundus the Second."

"You don't think . . . ?" Nyro began, staring in disbelief at the bowl in the center of the room.

"That it's your friend Luther's blood?" Osman finished the sentence for him.

Nyro nodded. "Or his mother's?" he whispered.

Osman frowned. "It could be either. On the other hand, it might just be animal blood. Let's hope so."

"But why would anybody bring a bowl of animal blood here?"

"I suspect that there's only one way to find out," Osman told him. "Could you just prop that mirror up against the far wall? But don't take the cover off. Just sit down in front of it for now."

Puzzled, Nyro did as Osman suggested. "What are you going to do?" he asked.

"It's what *you're* going to do that counts," Osman told him. He sat down cross-legged beside Nyro and took a stub of candle out of his pocket along with a box of matches. "In a moment," he continued, "I'm going to light this candle. Then I'm going to remove the cover from the mirror. When I do that, I want you to start talking about your friend Luther."

"Why?"

"Never mind why," Osman said. "Just do exactly as I tell you, and you won't be in any danger. Talk about things that matter to you—why Luther was your friend, why you are still looking for him now when everyone else has forgotten he ever existed. As you speak, I want you to keep looking in the mirror. Whatever you see there, it is very important that you take absolutely no notice of it. Do not even acknowledge its existence. Is that clear?"

"What do you expect me to see in this mirror?" Nyro said.

"I don't *expect* anything," Osman said more loudly this time, almost as if there were somebody else in the room who might be listening.

Nyro flinched. Osman's behavior was beginning to unnerve him.

Osman struck a match and lit the candle. "Are you ready to begin?" he asked.

"I think so."

"Good. Remember, speak the truth and leave nothing out. Do not stop unless I tell you to. Begin now!" Osman reached out and, with a flourish, removed the black velvet cloth from in front of the mirror.

Nyro began describing how he had first become friends with Luther. It had been during his first year at secondary school. He had not found it easy to make the transition from his tiny primary school, where everyone knew him, to the anonymity of a large secondary school. There had been a boy at the school called Joseph Brandon who had bullied him mercilessly. Nyro always did his best to stay out of Brandon's way, but one lunchtime, in search of peace and quiet, Nyro had wandered over to a partially hidden area behind some temporary classrooms—only to discover that Joseph Brandon and two of his henchmen were already there. As Brandon looked up and saw him, a grin spread across his face. He said something to his friends and they rapidly moved to block Nyro's retreat. Then Brandon grabbed him and pushed him up against the wall.

"What's the matter, mummy's boy? Are you scared?" Brandon mocked.

Nyro *had* been too scared to even reply.

"Leave him alone."

Brandon turned in surprise to see Luther standing, quite calmly, watching the scene.

"What's it got to do with you?" Brandon asked. He looked confident enough, but Nyro thought he detected a note of uncertainty in the bully's voice.

"He's my friend."

Nyro was astonished. He had scarcely even spoken to Luther.

Brandon hesitated, then shoved Nyro towards Luther. "Take him, then, if you're so keen on him!" he said.

It was an incident that Nyro recalled with the utmost clarity—and yet, as he described what had happened, he found it extremely difficult to put it into words. The parts that involved himself and Joseph Brandon were easy enough to describe. But as soon as Luther came into the picture, Nyro felt himself drying up. It was almost as if there was some external force preventing him from talking about Luther—something or someone who didn't want to hear his friend's name.

"Keep talking!" Osman urged.

Nyro began to speak about the day Luther had come up with the idea of going on a hiking trip. As he described how they had sat in Luther's bedroom, poring over a map of the wilderness that lay between Tavor and Gehenna, he began to be aware of a smell in the room, like something rotten, growing stronger by the minute.

In the mirror he noticed a shape now lurking in the background. The more Nyro talked, the clearer the shape became, until at last it was clearly visible—a figure crouching in the corner of the room. It was like a man, except that a pair of leathery wings stuck out from its shoulder blades. Its skin glistened with slime and its clothes hung around it in rags. With an expression of pure malevolence, it stared back at Nyro.

Horrified, Nyro was on the point of turning his head to tell Osman what he had seen, but the old man put out his hand and stopped him. "I know what you're going to tell me, Nyro," he said, speaking very slowly and deliberately. "You're going to tell me that you don't see anyone. Neither do I."

Nyro opened his mouth to protest, but Osman spoke first. "We're going to leave now," he said, "because it's all been a waste of time. There's nothing here for us to see. Come on."

He got to his feet, picking up the candle at the same time. "Take the mirror," he told Nyro, "and the cloth. We needn't have bothered with it at all, since there was nothing here to see."

Osman sounded as if he were speaking to a very young child or a foreigner who might not understand the language. As he led the way out of the room, he kept on repeating that there had been no one in the room, that they had seen absolutely nothing, that it had all been completely pointless.

Together they went down the stairs and out the front door. Only when they were standing in the street did Osman's manner change.

"Are you all right?" he asked.

"I think so," Nyro said, though his whole body was trembling and he was not sure his legs would support him much longer. "What on earth was that?"

"Let's not talk about it just now," Osman said. "We'd better go back to my house for a little while. I think you need some time to recover."

They crossed the road in silence while Nyro tried to make sense of what had just happened. He felt weak and light-headed and tainted, as if some of what he had just witnessed had rubbed off on him.

Osman made him sit in the kitchen while he made some kind of herbal tea. The butler, it seemed, had either gone home or gone to bed. The tea tasted disgusting, but Osman insisted that Nyro drink it all before he would even begin to discuss what they "hadn't" seen. As Nyro sipped the murky liquid, he felt himself growing rapidly stronger. "Okay," he said when he had finally consumed it all. "Now tell me what that was about."

"Very well," Osman said, sitting down opposite him. "The creature you just saw is called a sumaire. It is an elemental, which means that it does not really belong in our world."

"Then what's it doing here?"

"It's absorbing all traces of your friend."

"You mean it's because of that creature that everyone has forgotten about Luther?"

"Exactly."

Nyro considered this. "So if it doesn't belong in our world, how did it find its way into Luther's house?" he asked.

"It has been summoned here. Either by Brigadier Giddings himself, which seems unlikely given what you have told me about him, or by someone with whom he is in league. But there's no doubt that its appearance here has been deliberately contrived. That's why the Brigadier brought the bowl of blood. Sumara are attracted by blood."

"Do they drink it?" Nyro asked.

"No. But there is something about it that gives them pleasure. Perhaps it is an essence that blood gives off. I can't say for certain. The experts are all rather vague on this point."

"What experts?"

"The ancient writers. The sumara may have been forgotten in recent times, but only a few hundred years ago scholars discussed them regularly."

"How do you know so much about them?" Nyro asked suspiciously.

Osman shrugged. "Because I am interested in things that have been lost or hidden from the everyday world. That's why I have devoted so much time and energy to studying the work of Alvar Kazimir Mendini, as much of it as can still be found. You will recall that I mentioned his name earlier?"

"You said that Luther had come to a talk you gave about him."

"Exactly. Your friend was curious to learn more about the famous Canticle, of which only a few fragments still remain. Would you like to hear one of them?"

Nyro shook his head. "I'm not very interested in poetry."

"But you will be interested in this. Listen to the opening lines." Osman cleared his throat and began to recite in a deep, sonorous voice:

> "A house is waiting in the darkness,
> A bowl of blood upon the floor.
> In the mirror lies the doorway:
> Lose your name to find the door."

Nyro started at the reference to a bowl of blood. "Are you making this up?" he demanded.

"I can assure you, those are the exact words with which the Canticle opens. Mendini showed them to me himself. He crossed the border into Tavor secretly a very long time ago. He came with his wife so that she could have a baby in safety. While he was here, I met him and he talked about this poem."

"But what does it mean?" Nyro asked impatiently.

"If I had to venture an opinion," Osman replied, "I would say the poem is about you, or at least that part is."

"But I'd never even heard of Mendini until today!"

"Nevertheless," Osman replied, "you must admit, it sounds very much as though Mendini had this evening's little incident in mind. It has been claimed that he could see into the future. He didn't have his wife's powers, but he had his own abilities. Of course, there's one sure way to find out if you really are the subject of the poem." He looked directly at Nyro as he said this, and his eyes seemed to glitter with anticipation. "Unless you're too frightened, that is?"

"What do I have to do?" Nyro asked warily. He did not like the suggestion that he might be a coward.

"Just what it says in the poem," Osman replied. "Lose your name to find the door. That shouldn't be terribly difficult."

"The door into where?"

"The door into the sumaire's world, of course," Osman replied.

With the memory of that creature, covered in slime and stinking like death itself, still fresh in his mind, every instinct in Nyro's body told him that he ought to get up and walk out of the old man's house this very instant.

Instead he asked, "Why should I want to enter the sumaire's world?"

"Because that is where you will find your friend Luther," Osman replied. "Of course, it will be dangerous and difficult and frightening. But worth doing, all the same. Don't you think?"

Nyro hesitated, then nodded. "Yes, I do."

"Splendid!" Osman said, rubbing his hands together in satisfaction. "That's all settled, then. I'll see you here tomorrow night. In the meantime, you mustn't eat anything. Nothing at all, you understand?"

Nyro nodded.

"Oh yes, and wear a black coat. That's very important."

"Will it be cold?"

Osman smiled. "On the contrary. I think you'll find it rather hot."

"Then why do I need a coat?"

"Let's just call it a little insurance policy," Osman said. "Now off you go. I've got a great deal of reading to do before tomorrow. And make sure you get plenty of sleep. You're going to need all your strength for what you will face tomorrow."

THE FUNERAL OF DR. SIGMUNDUS

Bea sat on the bed in her tiny room in the Museum of the Leader and looked around her, bewildered. She could not understand what she was doing here. Surely all this was in the past? Surely she had escaped from this dreadful place, along with Seersha? They had hijacked a truck and driven across country to Moiteera, where they had met up with Albigen and rejoined the Púca. She could remember it all quite clearly. But if that was true, then what was she doing back in the museum?

She glanced around the room, and her eye fell on the carved wooden bird that stood on a shelf in the alcove opposite the bed. It had been a birthday present from Dante. She took it down from the shelf and held it between her hands. The feel of the wood was somehow comforting, as if she were drawing warmth from it.

What had happened to Dante? She remembered him coming to the museum and trying to talk to her, but she had refused to listen and instead had set off the alarm. Was that the last she had seen of him? No! He had appeared on the cliff top near Eden Park during the night of the storm. But her memory of that night was confused. There had been another youth who had looked just like Dante and wanted to kill her. Then Dante himself had appeared. At first she thought he had come to save her, but then he, too, had tried to kill her. She shuddered as she recalled this. Dante was her enemy now. Yes, that was right. He had taken the name of Sigmundus the Second. All right, then. But still . . . why was she back in her room in the Museum of the Leader?

Bea gazed again at the carved wooden bird. "What am I doing here?" she asked.

To her amazement the bird spoke in reply. "You are dreaming, Bea," it told her. And now it was a real live bird, and Bea had the distinct impression she had seen it before.

"You *have* seen me before," it told her. "It was I who rescued you on the cliff top."

Bea nodded.

"It wasn't Dante who tried to kill you," the bird continued. "It was his body, that is all. The real Dante separated from his body in order to survive."

"So where is the real Dante now?" Bea asked.

"The real Dante is inside of me."

Bea felt a surge of joy. Of course! She should have known! She opened her mouth to speak, but everything around her became blurred and confused. A moment later she was awake and lying in her sleeping bag on the ground inside one of the beehive huts. She struggled to remember what she had been dreaming, certain that it had been tremendously important. But it was like clutching at mist. The more she tried to remember, the more the details eluded her, until in the end there was nothing left at all.

After breakfast the Púca gathered in the meetinghouse. By now they had all heard about the television broadcast, and an air of profound gloom hung over them. But at a very deep level, Bea felt an odd sense of hope that was connected in some way with the dream she still could not remember. She listened with growing impatience as the discussion focused on the possibility of escaping across the border into Tavor. Some people said it could not be done; others insisted that it was their only option.

Finally, Bea could stand it no longer. "We can't just run away!" she said.

Everyone turned to look at her.

"Well, what do *you* suggest?" Albigen asked.

"We . . . we have to make a gesture of some kind," she told him.

"Such as?"

"How about an attack on the funeral?" Bea had no idea where this idea had come from. Nor did she have any real idea how to carry it out. But it seemed to her that she saw a tiny flame of belief flicker in the eyes that looked back at her from all around the room. So she plunged on, making up tactics as she spoke. "We know how to make smoke bombs, don't we?"

Heads nodded in agreement.

"So that's what we do. We fit them with timers. Then two or three of us go into Podmyn tomorrow. Each one carries a bomb. We get on one of the special buses and travel to Ellison, where we split up and place our bombs somewhere central. Afterwards we come back again on the bus."

"But what's the point?" asked Dobry, a tall, thin, dark-haired young man from the north of Gehenna. He was one of the patrol leaders, and many of the Púca took their cue from him.

"The point is that the whole country will be watching," Malachy said. He was new to the Púca and had been less affected by the death of their leader, Ezekiel. It was only a week since he and Dante had hijacked an airplane and flown to Eden Valley, where Malachy had been reunited with Seersha, his long-lost wife.

"Exactly!" Bea agreed. "They'll see that things aren't quite as cozy as they appear on the television broadcast."

"And what happens after that?" Dobry asked.

"I don't know," Bea admitted. "Maybe we just have to take it one step at a time."

"But can we really fight Dante? Albigen saw him stop time itself."

"That isn't Dante," Bea replied.

Dobry frowned. "What do you mean?"

Bea hesitated. She had no real idea what she meant. She had just found herself saying it because somewhere, deep within her, she felt that it was true. There was an expectant silence as they all waited for her to explain herself.

"It's because of Dante that I'm here. When I was locked away in the Museum of the Leader, he came and found me. Whoever it is that is now calling himself Sigmundus the Second, I refuse to accept that it's the real Dante. And you shouldn't, either."

Faces stared back at her in bewilderment.

"It doesn't matter whether you believe me or not," she continued. "Dante taught me one thing: you have to have the courage to live up to your dreams. And I'm going to keep on doing that, whatever else happens. So I'm going to Ellison by bus tomorrow, and I'm going to cause some trouble. Anyone else who wants to join me is welcome."

A lot of people shook their heads at this. They had wanted to hope, but Bea's vision and opinions were difficult for most of them to accept. In the end only Albigen and Maeve volunteered to go, and she suspected that they did so more because they did not want to see her acting on her own than because they were fully convinced by what she had said.

So the following morning the three of them drove into Podmyn. This time the town was full of people milling around and talking excitedly about the bewildering events that had overtaken their country. Many were dressed in their best clothes and sported black armbands. In the town square half a dozen rather ancient buses stood waiting to take them to Ellison to witness the funeral of their former leader and the swearing-in ceremony of his young successor.

Bea, Albigen and Maeve joined the line and boarded the last bus, which was already nearly full. Bea found herself sitting next to a plump middle-aged woman who immediately began talking as if they had known each other all their lives. She told Bea that she was a baker. She lived above her shop in the market square and had never been out of Podmyn before. She was very excited about the trip but also confused. "We've never heard anything about this new leader before," she said. "And he's so young. I do hope he'll be up to the job. They say that Dr. Sigmundus himself chose him, so I suppose he must be the right person. Dr. Sigmundus wouldn't make a mistake about something like that." She sighed. "I still can't believe he's dead, can you?"

Bea shook her head. "Not really," she admitted.

"I mean, obviously he had to die sometime," the woman continued, "but it's such a terrible shock after he's done so much for us all and we've come to depend on him. I'm not ashamed to say I wept bitterly when I heard the news."

Fortunately, the woman did not seem to need any response. She chattered on as the bus left Podmyn and headed north for Ellison, even mentioning that she was worried about her dog. Apparently she had left him in the yard and put food out for him.

"But the neighbors don't like him," she confided. "They say he barks too much." She glanced over her shoulder in case any of her neighbors might be listening. Bea nodded sympathetically. At least this nonstop stream of talk meant that she didn't have to answer any questions about her own life.

The nearer they got to Ellison, the denser the traffic became. It seemed as though all of Gehenna was descending on the capital.

49

Flustered-looking security guards struggled to prevent the roads from becoming completely gridlocked.

Eventually their driver found a place to park, the passengers disembarked and Bea, Albigen and Maeve went off in different directions.

Leader's Square was thronged with people of all kinds, many of them wearing the tall black hats that were used by the higher echelons of society for ceremonial occasions. A stage had been erected at one end, and musicians were playing solemnly next to giant television screens that had been set up to relay the ceremony to the crowds.

At the moment the screens were showing a coffin standing on a plinth in the middle of an empty room. On the floor of the room a six-pointed star had been painted. This was the infamous Star Chamber, from which Dr. Sigmundus had ruled Gehenna. Now, as Bea watched, a procession advanced towards the coffin. At its head, dressed in a long black robe and wearing a circle of gold upon his head, was Dante.

Bea watched as he and three other anonymous officials lifted the coffin onto their shoulders and began to carry it out of the room. As they did so, the name for the circle of gold on his head came to her. It was a crown: a word from her history books. Dante, or Sigmundus the Second as he preferred to call himself, was not just the ruler of Gehenna. He had made himself a king. Bea shook her head sadly. Although it seemed impossible to believe that these were the actions of her friend, she couldn't deny that the young man on the screens looked like Dante. How could she have insisted otherwise to her fellow Púca? What had she been thinking of?

Bea turned and made her way through the crowd towards the fenced-off area in front of the stage, where the musicians had deposited their instrument cases. Reaching inside the bag she carried, she pressed the timer switch that activated her smoke bomb. Then, as casually as she could, she dropped the bag over the guardrail, among all the equipment. She waited for a moment in case anyone had noticed, then began walking rapidly away. Suddenly, to her dismay, she heard her name being called. But her alarm gave way to confusion. She knew that voice!

Bea turned to see her father striding through the crowd towards her, his face lit up with a huge smile. As she recovered from her initial shock, she found that she felt quite suddenly like a little girl once again.

"Bea, how wonderful to see you!" her father exclaimed, putting his arms around her and hugging her tightly. "What on earth are you doing here?"

Bea could only shake her head. She knew that if she spoke, she would burst into tears.

Her father lowered his voice. "We thought you were in prison. We were told never to mention your name again. But I never gave up hope."

"I'm sorry, Dad." It was all Bea could manage.

Suddenly an idea seemed to occur to him. "Is it because of the new Leader?" he asked. "Is that why you're here?"

Bea nodded.

Her father looked even more delighted. "I knew it!" he said. "So many things are going to be different now. I've just got a promotion," he added. "I won't be based in Tarnagar anymore. I'm moving up north." He sounded almost like a little boy who has been praised by his teacher. Then he added something in a lower voice that she could not quite make out. Something like, "I'll be in charge of the Faithful."

"How's Mum?" Bea asked.

Her father's smile faded and enthusiasm drained from his face. "Of course. You weren't informed. Your mother and I separated after you were taken away." He sighed. "She felt I was to blame for what happened."

"Oh, Dad!" Bea said, feeling a stab of guilt. It was not her father's fault that her parents' marriage had broken up, whatever her mother might think. It was her own refusal to accept the world in which she had been raised. She had given them something to argue about.

"Never mind," her father said. "I think your mother's probably happier without me, anyway. Still, we did have some good times as a family, didn't we? Do you remember how we used to watch the stars together when you were young?"

When Bea was little, her father had ordered a telescope from the mainland and mounted it on the roof of their house. Night after night they had studied the skies together, and he had taught her the names of the constellations. It was something Bea had not thought about for a long time.

The memory of that innocent time was so poignant it was painful to even think about. Bea wanted to tell her father how much that experience had meant to her, but before she could say another word, shouting came from the direction of the stage, where clouds of smoke had begun billowing upwards. Moments later, two more columns of smoke rose in the air. A wave of panic surged through the crowd, and people began pushing backwards, separating Bea from her father. Soon she lost sight of him. Then a big man in an engineer's uniform shoved her roughly to one side so that she stumbled and fell to the ground. Within seconds people were trampling over her.

THE CIRCLE OF UNDOING

It was about five minutes before midnight, and they were standing in the alleyway behind Luther's house. Nyro had eaten nothing since their meeting the evening before, and he was feeling distinctly light-headed. He struggled to concentrate on what Osman was telling him.

"You have to make a circle of undoing," Osman repeated. "Crossing over into the sumara's world isn't going to be easy, you know. Things have to be done in the right order and in a way that the sumara will find acceptable."

"What happens if we get it wrong?"

Osman shook his head. "We will *not* get it wrong."

They climbed over the back fence, entered through the back door and made their way upstairs. Flies buzzed angrily around the bowl of blood, and the smell in the room had grown so bad that Nyro found himself gagging.

Calmly Osman opened the leather satchel he had been carrying, took out a mirror and placed it in the middle of the floor. Nyro saw that something was written on the mirror, but he could not make out the unfamiliar words. Next Osman took a paper bag and cut a hole in one corner to allow its contents—some sort of white powder—to trickle out. In this way he began to outline a large circle on the floor around the mirror.

"What is that stuff?" Nyro asked.

"Salt. It's a safeguard. A sumaire will not willingly cross a line of salt." Osman finished the circle and put the bag away. "Now take off your coat and give it to me."

Nyro did as he was told.

Osman put the coat on the ground, took a piece of chalk out of his pocket and, bending down, wrote in large letters on the back of the coat, ꟷ WISH OT SPEAK OT LUTHER.

"Just put your coat back on and hold out your left hand," Osman told him, standing up once more.

Nyro did as he was ordered, and Osman took a ball of string and tied one end around Nyro's left index finger. Finally he seemed satisfied with his preparations. "Now listen very carefully," he said. "For the purposes of this task, you must forget your own name. You will no longer be Nyro. Instead, you will be Oryn. When I tell you to, begin walking around the circle slowly in a clockwise direction. As you walk, repeat your new name. Say to yourself over and over again, 'My name is Oryn.' And try to believe it. You must do this ninety-nine times, without stopping. If you lose count, you must begin all over again.

"When you have completed the ninety-ninth circle, start walking backwards around the circle in the opposite direction. Do this once for every year of your life. Continue to tell yourself that your name is Oryn. When this is finished, move to the center of the circle, pick up the mirror and look at the face that you see. Ignore the writing. It will make no sense to you. Instead, concentrate on one thought only: that you are inside the mirror looking out. Continue to stare into the mirror until this thought becomes a reality. When that happens, you will know what to do next. Finally, if you feel you are in danger at any time, tug on the string. I shall have hold of the other end, and I will pull you back out of the circle of undoing and into the world you have left behind. Is that all clear?"

"It . . . is," Nyro said hesitantly.

"Excellent." Osman reached into the leather satchel once more and brought out a small drum. "Now walk!" he ordered.

As Nyro walked round the outside of the circle, Osman walked with him, holding the drum and the end of the string in one hand and beating the drum with the other. To begin with, Nyro felt a little self-conscious and faintly ridiculous. But as the ritual continued, he found his mind emptying of everything except the sound of the drum, the need to place one foot in front of the other, the process of keeping count and the thought that his name was Oryn. It was more tiring than he had expected. On the fifty-fifth circle, he stumbled slightly, but he regained his balance and strengthened his will. He did not want to have to start all over again.

After a while, as he told himself over and over again that his name was Oryn, it seemed that he was doing no more than stating the truth. That *was* his name. Perhaps it had always been his name. Yes, Oryn was his true identity. Whatever else he had called himself by in the past was nothing more than an illusion.

When he had completed the ninety-ninth circle, the drumbeat changed and he knew immediately what this meant: it was time to begin walking backwards sixteen times—one circle for each year of his life. As he did so, he began to understand more fully the purpose of the ritual. He was moving backwards through time to the point between life and . . . what? He grappled with the concept. To the point between life and the place where life came from, of course. That was his ultimate destination. That was why he was undoing himself—so that he might step through the doorway between this world and the larger one that lay behind it.

The drumbeat stopped. He had completed the sixteenth circle. His name was Oryn. He was no age at all. He had not yet been born.

He stepped across the line of salt, into the center of the circle, where he picked up the mirror and looked into its depths. His own face stared back at him, partially covered by the words that had been written in some obscure language: ꓄AOƆ ꓤUOY ꟻꟻO ƎꓘA꓄.

Briefly he tried to make sense of them, but they were in a tongue he had never encountered before. Instead, he concentrated on his reflection, and as he did so, he recalled someone a long time ago telling him a great secret. What was it? Ah! He was not the one looking into the mirror; he was the one within the mirror, looking out.

No sooner had he thought this than he found it was true. He was no longer looking into the mirror but looking out, and now he saw that the writing on the mirror was not incomprehensible at all. It was a simple message: TAKE OFF YOUR COAT, it read. Oryn put down the mirror and did as he had been ordered. As he held up the coat, he saw that another message had been written on its back in chalk: I WISH TO SPEAK TO LUTHER.

He was pondering the meaning of this when he became aware of the sound of someone else's breathing. Looking up, he saw a creature standing in the corner of the room. It looked like a man except for its leathery wings.

"Why have you come here?" the creature demanded. Its voice was like something that had bubbled up from the bowels of the earth, and when it spoke, it showed a mouthful of needle-like teeth.

But Oryn was ready with his answer. "I wish to speak to Luther," he said.

The flicker of a smile crossed the sumaire's face. "Very well," it said. "You shall have your wish."

It led the way out of the room, and after a moment's hesitation, Oryn put down the mirror and followed. As he did so, he felt a cold sensation in the index finger of his left hand. Looking down, he saw that a thin green light was unfurling endlessly from his fingertip towards the mirror. He wondered what it meant, but there was no time to waste thinking about this. If he was not careful, he would lose sight of his guide.

The sumaire had already descended to the floor below and was opening the front door. Quickly Oryn followed.

The first thing he noticed was the heat. It hit him like a wave, a dry heat that made his skin prickle. Then he began to take in his surroundings. The house was perched upon a rim of rock that ran in a circle around a vast crater. At scattered intervals along the rim there were other buildings: some no more than mud huts; some like the one he had just left; others much larger and grander, with great stone steps leading up to pillared entranceways, as if they were the palaces of kings or the parliaments of great nations. But this was not a city or a town, or even a village, for there was no sense of community among these dwelling places. Each building stood alone, as if it had been plucked from its rightful position and deposited here in secret, where it remained cut off from its neighbors and ashamed to be seen in such company.

"What is this place?" Oryn asked.

"This is the Nakara," the sumaire told him.

"And why are these buildings here?"

"They are the Lacunae—places that are neither fully part of your world nor fully part of mine. In each one a portal has been created, and that is how we travel between the worlds. But these are only the outskirts. You must come deeper into the Nakara if you wish to speak with your friend."

The sumaire began to lead the way around the rim of the crater. Above them the walls disappeared into dark purple clouds. Thunder rumbled menacingly, and from time to time the sky was lit up by forked lightning. Glancing over the edge, Oryn realized that the crater was far deeper than his sight could possibly fathom.

Now they came to a set of steps and began to descend steeply. The deeper they went, the hotter it grew. Other sumara flew back and forth across the crater, emitting raucous cries like giant birds, but Oryn's guide paid no attention to them. "Hurry up!" it kept telling Oryn. "We must go deeper!"

At last they found themselves on the next rim of the crater. A fierce, insistent wind blew constantly through the rows of twisted thorn trees, their leaves as gray as the bare rock from which they sprang. As Oryn drew nearer, a low moaning seemed to come from the trees themselves, a human sound and one so full of regret and disappointment that tears began to run down his cheeks.

The sumaire led the way through the trees, and soon Oryn understood why the sound had affected him so strongly. From the heart of each tree a face stared out at him with an expression of intense suffering.

"What are these creatures?" Oryn demanded.

The sumaire looked at him contemptuously. "Do you not recognize your own kind?" it asked. "Each of them was once like you. See, there is your friend Luther." It pointed to one of the trees that grew closest to the edge of the rim. Oryn went closer.

"Nyro, is that you?" said a voice from within the tree.

Oryn stared back at the tree in bewilderment. Softly he repeated the name by which it had addressed him. "Nyro." Yes, that was his name.

"Luther, what has happened to you?" he asked.

"This is my death," Luther told him. "It has taken the shape into which I grew during my life."

"I don't understand," Nyro said. "You weren't like this. You were a good person."

"You only knew me as I once was," Luther replied. "You did not see what I became at the end."

"But isn't there any hope that you might escape from this terrible place?"

"Not if the bridge across the abyss is built," Luther replied.

"What do you mean?" Nyro asked.

"A bridge is being built between the edge of the Nakara and the Resurrection Fields," Luther told him. "If it is completed, then all hope will die—for me, for you and for all mankind."

"Who is building this bridge?" Nyro asked.

"His name is Orobas," Luther replied.

As he spoke these words, there came an enormous clap of thunder. The ground beneath began to shake with increasing violence. A moment later the rock on which Nyro was standing tilted dramatically, and he lost his balance, fell down and began rolling towards the edge. Frantically he reached out for something to hold on to, but the ground beneath him shuddered once more, and he was shrugged off the rim to fall helplessly towards the depths of the crater.

At first his mind was filled with nothing but the sheer terror of his fall. But then he remembered Osman's instructions. There was no string attached to his finger now, but instead that strange green light unfurling endlessly from the tip of his index finger. He seized it with his right hand and pulled as hard as he could.

Back in Luther's room Osman was standing on the edge of the circle, watching Nyro carefully. He had been far from certain that the ritual would really work. Some of it he had pieced together from ancient manuscripts. The rest he had filled in himself, making an educated guess about what ought to happen next. It was clear that Nyro had entered a deep trance. But now, suddenly, he let out a yell and pulled hard on the string that ran between his index finger and Osman's.

Osman knew what he had to do. It was essential that he pull Nyro out of the circle without stepping into it himself. But he had time to do no more than think of this before he found himself yanked roughly towards Nyro. No sooner had he stepped inside the circle than the walls of Luther's room vanished and he was hurtling downwards.

"What a fool I've been to imagine I could exercise any control over this ritual!" he told himself. "I've meddled with things beyond my understanding."

THE RESURRECTION FIELDS

Bea struggled to get to her feet, but the panicking crowd would not let her rise. So instead she wrapped her arms around her head and curled up in a ball in an attempt to avoid being trampled to death. "This is how it ends," she thought, waiting for the blow that would knock her into unconsciousness.

But it did not come. Yet.

Or perhaps it came and she did not feel it? Perhaps this was what death was like? Then suddenly she was somewhere else entirely.

Scrambling to her feet, Bea looked around and found herself surrounded by a vast, grassy plain. Here and there a few trees dotted the landscape, but there was nothing else except a line of blue hills in the distance. A few yards away to her right, the ground was shifting and rippling. Then, a moment later, a shower of earth was flung upwards, and she realized with a gasp that something was digging its way out.

A human hand pushed through the soil, then another, followed by a man's head. Like a dog drying itself after swimming, the digger shook the dirt from his face and then proceeded to clamber out of the hole he had made. He was quite young, in his mid-twenties probably, and completely naked. Despite the mud with which his muscular body was streaked, it was clear that he was strikingly handsome. He gazed in Bea's direction with an expression of complete serenity while she stared back at him, shocked and confused. But either her presence did not surprise him or he simply did not notice her, because a moment later he turned without acknowledging her existence and began walking away towards the distant hills.

Bea opened her mouth to call, but she was interrupted as the ground from which the young man had emerged now began to move of its own accord once more. Like melting chocolate, the individual lumps of earth, and even the grass that grew on them, began to flow together and coalesce so that within a short time the area had returned to its former undisturbed condition.

A little way to her right, the earth was being thrown into the air once more. A middle-aged woman emerged naked and dirty but smiling beatifically before wandering off into the distance. Before long the hole from which she had climbed had also covered itself up, and not far away another individual was clawing his way to the surface. As Bea stood there in mute disbelief, more and more people sprang from the ground—tall, short, skinny, heavy, muscular, bony, dark-skinned, light-skinned. It was as if they were a crop that had been planted and was now maturing all at once. Bea had seen some extraordinary things since leaving Tarnagar, but nothing had prepared her for this.

Feeling something touch her on the shoulder, she spun around and saw a winged man dressed in a long white robe standing beside her. He was tall with shoulder-length hair, and he glowed with a light that seemed to come from within his body.

"Tzavinyah!" she gasped, for she had seen him once before on the night that Ezekiel had been killed.

"Beatrice," he said.

She had always insisted on being called Bea by everyone else, including her parents, ever since she was old enough to have an opinion on the matter. But she would not have dared to correct Tzavinyah, who seemed to possess an authority more complete than any she had ever encountered.

"I have been calling you for many days," he told her, and she was immediately transported by the icy beauty of his voice. "But your sadness has made you deaf to me."

"I'm sorry."

"It could not be helped. You are here now. That is what matters."

"But what is this place?" Bea asked.

"These are the Resurrection Fields," Tzavinyah replied. "It is where those who have encountered death find their way to a new life."

"You mean all these people are dead?"

"Once. Certainly."

"Does that mean that I'm . . . ?"

Tzavinyah shook his head. "You came in response to my summons. They arrived here by a longer path. Watch them. Try to see where they go."

Bea did as he suggested, but however hard she tried to watch any of the figures that emerged from the earth, there was always a point at which she found she looked away, without even being aware she had done it. And when she looked back, the figure had disappeared, though another was busily digging its way to the surface nearby.

Tzavinyah smiled. "You cannot see where they go," he told her, "and it is no different for me. Some things are hidden from all of us. All we know for certain is that this is where they begin their new journey."

"But I don't understand. If I'm not dead, then why have you brought me here?" Bea asked.

"Turn around," Tzavinyah replied.

Bea did as she was told and saw that behind her the plain stopped abruptly as if a giant knife had sliced through it. Beyond the edge was a pale blue nothingness that was neither sky nor cloud nor even air.

"Behold the abyss!" Tzavinyah said. "It lies between the Nakara and the Resurrection Fields. Now look through the telescope."

Beside them, on a stand, was a telescope similar to the one that Bea and her father had used for stargazing when she had been a child. Bending down, she looked through the eyepiece. At first she could see nothing but a vague blue blur. But as she turned the focusing knob, a picture began to emerge of what was happening on the other side of the abyss.

"What do you see?" Tzavinyah asked.

"It looks as though someone is building a bridge," Bea replied.

Tzavinyah nodded gravely. "You gaze upon the edge of the Nakara. The bridge that you see is the work of Orobas. But he must not be allowed to succeed."

"Who is he?" Bea asked.

"He is our enemy," Tzavinyah told her. "Yours and mine and every living creature's. In my tongue his name means hunger, and in truth that is all he is—an appetite that can never be satisfied, an emptiness that can never be filled. He must be stopped, and you are the one who must do it."

"Me? How can I stop him?"

Tzavinyah gave a slight sigh. It was a sound that filled Bea with so much sadness that she felt as if she would never be glad again. "As I told you, some things are hidden from all of us," he said. "The path of our enemy's defeat is just such a thing. I do not know what you must do, only that no one else can do it."

"But how will I know what to do?" Bea asked.

"I cannot say," Tzavinyah said. "But your task may be more

obvious than you think. Sometimes the answer is right in front of us though we cannot see it for looking. My advice is this: look for the hardest choice, the one that everyone seeks to dissuade you from. That is the path you must choose."

There were so many more things Bea wanted to ask, but instantly the scene began to grow faint. Once more she began to hear the shouts and cries of a panicked crowd. In the blink of an eye, she was again curled up on the ground in Leader's Square while people surged past, driven frantic by the smoke that billowed all around them. Boots thudded into her ribs as people stumbled across her. Somebody kicked her on the head, and the pain arched through her like a lightning bolt.

Suddenly she felt someone grip her arm and pull her to her feet. "Are you all right?" Albigen asked.

"I think so."

"Come on, we have to get out of here!"

ENIL'S TREE

It took Kidu over a week to recover, a week during which Dante turned over and over in his mind the words that his mother had whispered to him in that panic-stricken moment before he had fled the Odylic realm.

On Enil's Tower there is a message for Bea.

He did not dare to return to the Odylic realm to ask his mother what she meant. Orobas would be waiting for him, like a wild beast prowling outside the mouth of the cave where its prey has sought refuge.

In the meantime, he kept thinking about the black hole that Kidu called Shurruppak. Dante pressed Kidu to explain what he meant.

"Story of Shurruppak is story of beginning of world," Kidu said, as if this explained everything.

"But I don't know about the beginning of the world," Dante replied.

For a long time Kidu refused to accept this, insisting that Dante was trying to trick him, but eventually he was persuaded to tell the story of how all things began, as he had learned it in the nest.

"First of all was Anki, mother of all zimbir," Kidu told Dante. "Feather fall from Anki's wing. Become the world. Sun, moon, stars, land and sea—all grow from Anki's feather. Then Iggigi appear. Mate for Anki. Anki lay egg. Egg hatch. Shurruppak come out. Eat and eat and eat. Anki cannot feed him. Ask Iggigi, 'What shall we do?' Iggigi cover him with darkness of night. Shurruppak

66

silent but not finished. Just waiting. Meantime, Anki lay more eggs. Many new zimbir hatch. Different tribes. Kekkaka—Kidu's tribe. Huwawa with curved beaks. Others, too. Many, many tribes. All live together. Happy time in Nirnasha."

"Nirnasha?" Dante asked.

"Home Above the Sky," Kidu told him impatiently. "Kidu can't tell story if Giddim ask questions."

"Sorry," Dante said. "Please go on."

Kidu paused for a long time, to make it clear that he was not prepared to tolerate any more interruptions. But at last he deigned to continue. "Time not stay happy. Zimbir begin to fall out. Huwawa worst of all. Kill their brothers and sisters. Anki find out. Very angry. All zimbir thrown down to earth. Path back to Nirnasha hidden from them. Anki say, 'From now on every zimbir make a thousand journeys before him find Hidden Path.'"

The thought of how the zimbir had been thrown out of paradise for preying upon one another seemed to fill him with sadness, and he sat without moving for hours on end so that Dante had to persuade him to find insects to eat in order to keep up his strength.

"Remember, you have seen the Hidden Path," Dante reminded him, when Kidu still seemed gloomy the following day. "It hasn't disappeared."

"But will Kidu see it again before Shurruppak eats it?" Kidu replied unhappily. "Maybe not."

"Tell me the rest of the story," Dante coaxed, and eventually Kidu agreed.

"Everything different after zimbir leave Nirnasha," he began. "Every day new creatures born out of dirt. First small, like muzur. Then bigger. Last and worst is zittenziteen. Aaach! Terrible creature. Walk on two legs. No fly. Full of noise. Make traps for zimbir. Fight all creatures. Soon Anki grow angry once more. Say, 'Let Shurruppak eat up everything.' But Iggigi say, 'No. I have plan. Zittenziteen is most cunning creature. Find strongest one. Make him ruler over all. Even zimbir. Then we get peace.' So Anki and Iggigi fly over world. Look for strongest zittenziteen. Find Enil."

"Wait a minute!" Dante interrupted. "Did you say his name was Enil?"

On Enil's Tower there is a message for Bea.

"Giddim want to hear story, Giddim listen!" Kidu said.

"Sorry."

"Giddim always sorry. Not good enough! Bad as zittenziteen!"

"Sor—I mean, please carry on."

"Kidu forget what happening."

"Iggigi and Anki found Enil."

"Oh yes! Now Iggigi tell Enil, 'Make other zittenziteen behave. Or Anki let Shurruppak eat up everything.' Enil agree. At first everything good. Zittenziteen stop trapping zimbir. All creatures stop fighting. Iggigi visit Enil often. Enil build stone tree for him to land on."

A stone tree! Enil's Tower. It had to be!

"But other zittenziteen jealous," Kidu continued. "One day they put poison in Enil's food. Enil fall asleep and stay asleep. Right away everything turn bad again. Zittenziteen make traps. Huwawa kill their brothers and sisters. Even muzur fighting. Anki look down and see what going on. 'Enough!' she say to Iggigi. 'Your plan no good. Now I send Shurruppak to eat up everything, even Hidden Path.' " Kidu sighed. "Iggigi want to help zimbir. He promise to send Zimbir That Is Not Zimbir, show the way back to Hidden Path."

"Zimbir That Is Not Zimbir—what does that mean?" Dante asked.

"Kidu not know. No one know. Maybe Iggigi forget his promise because now Shurruppak has come," he concluded miserably.

"Tell me more about Enil," Dante urged.

"Nothing else to tell," Kidu replied irritably. "Only good zittenziteen ever. Others poisoned him."

"What about the stone tree that he built for Iggigi to perch on?"

"What about it?"

"Is it still standing?"

"Of course!"

"Can we go there?"

"Kidu not fall for same trick twice. Giddim promise Kidu to go away if Kidu show him Shurruppak. Then he say sorry, can't go. Giddim always sorry. Kidu not want to fly to Enil's tree. Waste of time."

"Listen, Kidu. I *do* want to leave and I will, as soon as I can, but first I have a job to do. And part of that job involves defeating Shurruppak. That's what you want as well, isn't it?"

"Giddim defeat Shurruppak? Impossible!"

"Didn't I show you the Hidden Path?"

"Yes," Kidu conceded.

"You see, I have more power than you think. And I have a plan."

Kidu snorted. "Like Iggigi's plan?"

"Better than Iggigi's plan because this one is going to work. But first I need you to show me Enil's tree."

Kidu sighed. "No peace! No rest! All right, Giddim. Kidu show you Enil's tree. But then you make Shurruppak go away. Or . . ." He paused. "Or Kidu fall from Enil's tree. Keep wings still. End of Kidu. End of Giddim, too. Understand?"

"I understand."

* * *

A few days after the funeral of Dr. Sigmundus, Bea was sitting with her back to the stone pillar, trying to make sense of all that had happened. First there had been the meeting with her father. She could not forget the look on his face when he caught sight of her. She had disappointed him, she realized that, but he still loved her dearly. And she loved him, too, though they were on separate sides. Then there was the appearance of Tzavinyah. She had told the others about him and the things he had told her, but no one knew what to make of it.

Somebody coughed and she turned to see a pale youth of about her own age. Dark hair hung low over his forehead, and he was dressed in the uniform of a junior doctor on Tarnagar.

Startled, she scrambled to her feet. "What are you doing here?" she demanded.

He treated her to a rather unpleasant smile. "I've come to see you, of course. But I see you're looking at my uniform," he added. "I'm going to be promoted soon."

Bea stared back at him. His words echoed those her father had used at the funeral of Dr. Sigmundus. Had her father reported their meeting to the authorities? But why would they have sent a junior doctor to confront her?

The young man clasped his hands together and held them out in front of him. "Let's play a game," he said. "See if you can guess what I've got in my hand."

Bea could still only stare at him in confusion.

"Don't tell me you don't want to play," the young man said mockingly. "Oh well. I'll have to show you, then." He opened his hands, and Bea saw that a capsule of Ichor rested in the middle of his palm. "Recognize it?" he asked.

"What do you mean?"

"Oh, come on," he continued. "You're not going to try and tell me this isn't the capsule you flushed down the toilet in the Museum of the Leader?"

This was too much. Bea felt her grip on reality beginning to slip completely. "Who are you?" she demanded.

The youth frowned. "Let me see. Regret, recrimination, discontent, disappointment, disillusion. Are any of those names?"

"Of course not!" Bea replied.

"Then you can call me Set instead. It's much simpler."

"Look, what do you want?" Bea said.

"I've come for our wedding," he told her.

With that, Bea suddenly found herself standing in a Dagabo surrounded by a crowd of people, all wearing their best clothes. Among them were her mother and father and her classmates from Tarnagar. She was wearing a white wedding dress and facing the Official Receiver. Beside her was Set, smiling broadly and holding a ring between his finger and thumb.

Frantically she turned and tried to flee, but arms reached out to grab her, and a moment later she found herself being carried above their heads, screaming and struggling, along a series of corridors. Bea knew where she was now—in the asylum on Tarnagar. A moment later the crowd carried her into the Shock Room, the very chamber where she had witnessed Dante being tortured. Now she was pushed onto the chair and strapped in place. Electrodes were placed on her head—and then, with a searing jolt, she felt the most terrible pain rack her body.

When the pain stopped, Set was standing in front of her with one eyebrow raised quizzically. "If you want me to turn it off," he told her, "you must promise to be mine. It's as simple as that."

Bea shook her head. This time she thought the pain had killed her. But when she opened her eyes, there was Set once more.

"I'll tell you what," he said brightly. "I'll make it easy for you. You can promise to marry me only if the sky is filled with feathers and the moon sleeps in a basket. What do you say?"

"All right," Bea agreed desperately.

"That's a good girl," Set said. Then, quite suddenly, he vanished. And Bea found that she was lying on the ground beside the pillar.

So it had been a nightmare after all? And yet it had seemed so real! Feeling extremely weak, Bea propped herself up on her elbow. She then spotted a little bird perched on the steps of the pillar. It was so close that she could have reached out her hand and touched it. Yet it did not fly away. It didn't even seem to be afraid of her, just sat there quite calmly, looking at her with bright eyes.

The bird was white, like the one that had flown at Dante when he had tried to strangle her on the cliff top near Eden Valley. But it couldn't be the same bird, could it? All birds of a particular species looked more or less the same. But there *was* something odd about this one, the way it just sat there and stared at her as if it wanted to speak to her. Something stirred in her memory, some fragment of a dream, but she could not bring it to the surface.

"What do you want?" Bea asked.

The bird made no reply.

"Now you're just being ridiculous," Bea told herself. The nightmare had unnerved her. She really ought to go back and join the rest of the Púca. Help with preparing the food. That would bring her back to her senses. But the feeling that she ought to remember something held her there.

* * *

It had taken most of the afternoon to fly here, but as soon as Dante had caught sight of the stone pillar on the mountaintop, he had been certain that this was where his mother had meant him to come. No sooner had he spotted the pillar, however, than he saw Bea lying on the ground with a man standing beside her. The man had his back to Dante, but there was something distinctly familiar about him—something that made Dante extremely uneasy. Then, quite suddenly, he disappeared.

Moments later Kidu landed on the steps of the pillar. Bea did not move at first, and Dante was frightened that she might be dead. But then she opened her eyes and noticed Kidu.

"What do you want?"

If only Dante could find some way to let her know that he was there, in the body of the bird. But Kidu was already growing impatient.

"Well, Giddim, you see Enil's tree. Now you satisfied?" the bird demanded.

On Enil's Tower there is a message for Bea.

But looking out through Kidu's eyes, Dante couldn't see anything written on the pillar.

Kidu began tearing at the moss that grew on the stone step, seeking out the tiny insects that sheltered among its roots. He seemed to have found a particularly tasty variety, for he pecked away industriously, occasionally mumbling to himself.

"No, no, no, little muzur. Not run away from Kidu! Too slow! Too slow! Kidu eat you all up. Mmm! Very nice, very nice."

Dante did his best to ignore Kidu's enthusiasm. Sharing the bird's brain for so many days, he had soon learned to shut himself off from the physical sensations that accompanied Kidu's

73

mealtimes—the tiny but frantic struggle as the insect was seized in the bird's beak and swallowed whole, the delight Kidu took in catching his prey.

Suddenly Dante noticed that where the bird had pulled away the moss, letters had been carved into the stone.

"Pull up more moss!" Dante urged.

"Kidu not hungry now! Plenty muzur already!"

"You *must* pull up more moss!"

"Not *must*! Kidu please Kidu!" It was clear that Kidu was highly offended and in no mood to compromise. "Giddim always saying must do this, must do that," he went on. "Never say please, Kidu. Never say nice Kidu."

"I'm sorry."

"Giddim always sorry."

"Please, Kidu, pull up more of the moss. It's important if you really want to defeat Shurruppak."

"How pull up moss defeat Shurruppak? Giddim not make sense!"

"You have to trust me."

"Trust Giddim! Why?"

"Didn't I save you from the huwawa?"

"Save yourself as well."

"Yes, that's true. But I promise you that pulling up the moss will help defeat Shurruppak. Not right away, maybe, but soon."

Kidu hesitated. Dante could feel him considering whether to agree or not.

"I am very grateful to you for everything you've done so far," Dante told him. "Telling me the story of the beginning of all things, bringing me here."

"Showing you Shurruppak," Kidu reminded him.

"Yes, of course, showing me Shurruppak."

"Fighting zittenziteen."

Dante had to think about this for a moment. Of course, Kidu meant the time that he had flown at Dante's own body when Orobas had been using it to try to kill Bea. Dante was tempted to point out that this had not been something Kidu had done willingly. Dante had just forced him into it. But he wisely decided to keep this observation to himself.

"Yes, fighting the zittenziteen as well. You've been very, very good, Kidu. I realize that I'm always asking for favors, but I really *am* trying to defeat Shurruppak and leave your body, so if you would just be kind enough to tear away some more of the moss, I'd be so grateful."

Kidu hesitated. "Very well," he said at last. He bent down, ripped up another section of moss and immediately began pecking at the frantic insects that were exposed to the light of day.

At last Bea seemed to notice that something odd was going on. She stood up and moved closer. Immediately Kidu spread his wings and flew a little way off. Nothing that Dante could say would persuade him to get too close to a zittenziteen. But Bea herself was pulling at the moss by now and frowning as she tried to make sense of what was written underneath. Dante could not see what the letters said, but he could tell from Bea's reaction that they were making a deep impression on her. A moment later she turned and ran back towards the beehive huts, calling out excitedly to the others.

THE CHIEF JUSTICE

Relief flooded through Nyro as he felt an answering pull on the ribbon of green light that unfurled endlessly from his finger. His fall through the air came to an abrupt halt.

"I knew Osman would get me out of here!" he said to himself. "I knew he wouldn't let me fall!"

But just as suddenly the resistance at the other end of the line vanished completely, and he plunged downwards once again. The farther he fell, the darker it became until now he could see nothing at all. He closed his eyes and tried not to think about the pain he would experience upon impact. Curiously enough, he felt no anger with Osman for getting him into this, only a deep sadness that he was going to die so young without tasting fully what life had to offer.

Suddenly he made contact with the ground. At least that was what it felt like to begin with. Except that he kept falling, though now much more slowly. He opened his eyes to see what was happening, but everything was black. Then with a jolt he hit the bottom. He tried to cry out but immediately felt himself choking as his mouth filled with . . . with what? Mud? He must have fallen into a great pit of slimy muck. He closed his mouth again and frantically began flailing about as he tried to force his way upwards. More than once he felt like giving up, but instinct drove him on.

Suddenly he broke through to the surface, coughing and spluttering. As he did so, another shape plunged into the swamp and disappeared beneath its surface, causing great waves of muck to toss Nyro's body about like a cork on the ocean.

His eyes were beginning to adjust to the darkness now, and he could make out a tiny glimmer of light moving about to one side. He decided to head towards it. The trick, he realized after some time, was to make slow, careful movements with his arms and legs. In this way, he began to move steadily across the swamp.

He was still swimming when, with a great belch, the swamp propelled another figure onto the surface. It was too dark for Nyro to see who it was, but a moment later Osman's voice called out for help.

"This way!" Nyro shouted. "Try not to splash."

By now he had reached a part of the swamp that was shallow enough to stand up in, and it was much easier to make his way onto the shore, though the slime continued to pull at his legs with sucking noises, almost as if it were a living thing.

When he finally reached dry land, he lay down, utterly exhausted. He didn't care what happened now. At least he was out of that swamp. After a while he heard Osman getting closer, and eventually he stumbled over towards Nyro and collapsed on the ground behind him.

"What sort of place is this?" Osman asked when he could finally muster breath enough to speak. He peered about them in the gloom.

"You're supposed to be the expert," Nyro pointed out. "It was following your instructions that brought us here, remember?"

"Yes, well, the ancient scholars had plenty of ideas about how to reach the sumara's realm, but none of them told you what you might expect to find on the other side," Osman admitted.

"How come you didn't mention that before?"

"I didn't want to worry you."

"How very considerate."

"All right," Osman conceded, "I admit, this whole adventure may have been a little reckless, but things could have turned out a great deal worse. We are both still alive, after all."

"But we stink, in case you haven't noticed."

"Indeed we do," Osman agreed. "However, there's nothing to be gained by dwelling upon it." He got to his feet. "I think we should go and investigate that little light over there."

The light turned out to be an old-fashioned lantern with a candle inside. The most filthy and ragged-looking specimen of humanity that Nyro had ever come across held it aloft. Scarcely more than a skeleton, he was clad in a loose robe that came down to his bare feet. This unflattering garment must once have been white but was now a uniform gray and hung in tatters around the hem. The crown of his head was bald, but there was hair at the back and sides that had grown long and hung in greasy locks about his shoulders. He had an immense gray beard, and his eyebrows seemed to have decided to compensate for the lack of hair on the top of his head by sprouting wildly in all directions. As Osman and Nyro approached, he was kneeling down, peering keenly at the ground by the light of his lantern and muttering to himself. "That's seventy-six, I think. Yes, I'm sure it's seventy-six, or was it seventy-five? Yes, that's it, seventy-five. Ah! There's another one."

With that, he picked up something and placed it in a bowl on the ground beside him.

"Now then, that's seventy-six. Or is it seventy-seven?" he continued. "Better count them all again." He put down the lantern and picked up the bowl.

"Excuse me, sir?" Osman began.

But the old man was so startled he dropped the bowl. "No! No! No!" he moaned. "Now I've gone and spilled them all!"

"I sincerely apologize for alarming you," Osman told him. "I merely wanted to inquire whether you could tell my friend and me the best way out of this place."

But the old man took no notice of Osman's question. Instead, he tore at his hair and continued to moan pitifully. "Now I have to start all over again!" he complained.

"What exactly are you doing?" Nyro asked.

"Picking up the seeds!" the old man said impatiently. With that, he turned away from them and began scrabbling about on the ground.

Osman considered this for a moment. "Perhaps if we were to help you with your task, you might show us the way out in return," he suggested.

The old man looked up and nodded his head eagerly. "Yes, yes!" he said. "You help me. I help you. But hurry! There's no time to waste."

Nyro and Osman looked at each other and shrugged. Then they got down on their hands and knees and studied the little patch of ground illuminated by the feeble light of the lantern.

"How many seeds are there?" Nyro asked.

"Nine hundred and ninety-nine," the old man replied.

"You'll never find that many!" Nyro exclaimed.

The old man stopped searching for a moment and turned two terrified, bloodshot eyes on Nyro. "I *have* to find them all," he said, "before he comes back."

"Before who comes back?"

The old man put his face right up close to Nyro's, so close that Nyro could smell his rotten breath.

"My tormentor," the old man whispered. Then he frowned and looked from Osman to Nyro and back again. He jerked his thumb in Osman's direction. "Is he your tormentor?" he asked.

Nyro was tempted to make a joke but suspected that the

old man would not appreciate it. So he simply said, "I haven't got one."

The old man seized Nyro's arm with one bony hand, gripping it so tightly that Nyro winced. "*Everyone* has a tormentor," the old man said. "You just haven't met him *yet*." With these words he released Nyro's arm and went back to scrabbling about on the ground. Nyro and Osman got down beside him and began searching for seeds.

It was tedious work and Nyro's knees soon began to ache. "How do you know there are nine hundred and ninety-nine?" he asked.

A tear ran down the old man's cheek at this question. "It is the number of my shame," he replied.

"What do you mean?"

"When I was alive—I mean truly alive, not like this—I was a man of great importance. I know you may find that hard to believe, but people quaked when they were brought before me, for I was the Chief Justice of Shinar, and I held their lives in the palm of my hand. If I ordered their release, they were released; if I ordered their death, they were put to death. There was no argument and no appeal. My judgment was final.

"I enjoyed that power. I liked to savor the look on the faces of the accused while they waited for my verdict. One day, because I was feeling particularly irritable that morning, I condemned a man to death even though I knew him to be innocent. I did it because he did not show me enough respect. I felt no remorse afterwards. In fact, I was rather pleased with myself. It would serve as an example to the others, I decided. That was the first time an innocent person died because of me, but it was not the last. In the years that followed, nine hundred and ninety-eight more joined him. It would have been a thousand, but I woke up one morning to find that instead of lying in my bed between silk sheets, I was here, and standing before me was my tormentor."

As he mentioned his tormentor, the old man began to shake. Nyro gently took the bowl from him and set it down on the ground. Then, silently, the three of them returned to searching the ground.

It was hard to say how much time passed as they crawled around in the darkness on their hands and knees, but at last there was only one more seed left to find.

"Here it is!" Nyro said. He picked up the seed and placed it carefully in the bowl with the others.

"Thank you, thank you," the old man muttered. "Now I will finally be released." He turned to Osman. "He promised, you know. He said if I could show him all nine hundred and ninety-nine in the bowl, he would let me go. They can't go back on a promise. Even *they* have to abide by some rules."

"Of course they do," Osman said reassuringly. "Now perhaps you wouldn't mind keeping your side of the bargain and showing us how we might get out of here."

"Very well," the old man agreed, "but first swear you will tell no one who showed you."

"We swear."

"Because if my tormentor should hear about it . . ."

"He won't hear about it."

"All right, then, follow me. Quickly now!"

He made his way around the base of the cliff, looking over his shoulder all the time and hissing at them to hurry. Finally he stopped at the entrance to a large tunnel. "This is the only way in or out. You must take the right fork. But hurry! He will be here soon."

They thanked him and entered the tunnel. Surprisingly, it was not completely dark, for the walls seemed to give off a dim light of their own. Almost as soon as they were inside, the tunnel branched in two directions. They stepped into the right-hand fork. Not a moment too soon! Out of the other fork came a sumaire. Fortunately, it was rushing ahead and did not notice them.

"That must be the old man's tormentor," Nyro whispered.

Just then they heard the most enormous sneeze from beyond the mouth of the tunnel and, immediately afterwards, the old man's despairing cry: "No! No! The seeds!"

THE TRAITOR

Manachee, Maeve and Albigen stared at the letters that had been carved in the stone step:

> *When every other hope has fled,*
> *When he is lost who once was found,*
> *Climb the stairs and greet the dawn,*
> *Make the world's most ancient sound.*

As he watched them, Dante felt his hopes begin to rise. Perhaps now that Bea had told them how a bird had helped her discover the message, it might be possible to find some way to communicate with them. Dante urged Kidu to move closer to the steps, and Kidu reluctantly hopped a few paces forward.

"There's the bird that scratched away the moss," Bea said. "I'm sure it was doing it on purpose."

Dante tried to persuade Kidu to move closer still, but the bird refused to cooperate. Bea took a couple of steps towards him, and Kidu immediately flew off to a nearby tree. Nothing Dante could say would persuade him to get any closer.

Bea turned back to the others. "I've got a feeling about this inscription," she told them. "Almost as if I was meant to find it. Do you think it was carved by the people who built the beehive huts?" she asked.

Manachee shook his head. "No. The language is far too modern. They lived long ago and spoke a much more ancient version of our tongue. We wouldn't be able to read their writing so easily."

"Then who put it there?"

"Anyone could have carved it. These steps have been here for hundreds of years. Thousands, maybe. Who knows how many people have come and gone in that time?"

"But you said people had forgotten their history since Dr. Sigmundus came to power. You said no one came here anymore."

"Yes, that's true. But perhaps someone put it there before Dr. Sigmundus was even born. On the other hand . . ." He hesitated.

"What?"

"We do know one person who came here regularly."

"Alvar Mendini?" Bea said eagerly.

"That's right. Like I said before, he used to come here to seek inspiration for his poetry. If I had to make a wild guess, I would say that this is a fragment of the Mendini Canticle."

"Do you really think that's possible?" Albigen asked.

"Alvar was no ordinary man," Manachee replied. "I knew him well, and I promise you, he could see things that had not yet happened. He might have left this message here many years ago, knowing that Bea would one day be standing here to read it."

"What *is* the Mendini Canticle?" Bea asked.

"The Mendini Canticle was Alvar's last poem," Manachee said. "But it was more than just a set of verses. He put all his powers into it, and all that he had learned of the Odylic realm from his wife, Yashar. He only ever really talked about it once to me, but I can still remember the words he used because they seemed so strange at the time. 'Long after I am dead,' he told me, 'my poem will still be taking place in the flight of a bird, in the actions of the Púca and in the mysterious workings of the Odyll. I have woven in events that are yet to happen, for my poem is alive and will let itself be known when it sees fit.' "

"The flight of a bird!" Bea repeated wonderingly.

"I agree it's a possibility," Albigen conceded. "But even so, what are we supposed to do about it?"

"I don't know," Manachee admitted. "But if this really is a fragment of the Mendini Canticle, then its meaning will become apparent when the time is right."

"And in the meantime," Albigen said, "we need to find out what's going on in Podmyn. We've had reports that there's a big event planned there this afternoon. Anyone want to come with me to take a look?"

"I will," Manachee said.

"So will I," Bea volunteered. Reluctantly she walked away from the pillar, still puzzling over the meaning of the verse.

Later that day Albigen drove them to Podmyn. Immersed in their own thoughts, they each had different ideas about what the Púca ought to be doing next, and it was becoming clear that they did not always see eye to eye. Without a leader to decide among them, tensions were beginning to simmer beneath the surface.

Albigen was, in many ways, the most obvious choice to lead the Púca following the death of Ezekiel Semiramis. He was strong, brave and quick-witted. But he was best at practical things. What he lacked was Ezekiel's vision and, more importantly, his powers. Manachee was one of the most senior members of the Púca, but he was a born second-in-command. That left Bea. As a newcomer, she should not even have been a candidate. Yet, since she had told the Púca of Tzavinyah's appearance, many of them held her in a kind of awe. Bea was not particularly comfortable being in this position, but Tzavinyah's words had been very clear—only she could overcome their enemy. If that meant taking control of the Púca, then she was prepared to do so.

"Let's stop the truck here," Albigen said. "We could leave it in one of those abandoned farm buildings up ahead."

With the increasing security presence since the funeral, it was wiser not to attract attention by driving a large truck right into the town. So they turned onto the farm track and parked the truck inside an empty barn, making the rest of the journey to Podmyn on foot.

The small town was full of people. However, unlike the day of Dr. Sigmundus's funeral, when farmworkers had proudly put on their best clothes and chatted freely, this time people were keeping their thoughts to themselves, glancing about nervously and talking in low voices. It was clear that a swirl of rumor had the whole place in its grip.

"I wonder what they're so worked up about," Bea said.

"Looks like we're going to find out shortly," Albigen replied, nodding towards a wooden platform that had been assembled in the town square. As they watched, a security officer climbed a set of steps at the side of the platform and held up one hand for the crowd to be silent. Almost immediately the buzz of conversation ceased and several hundred anxious faces looked up at him expectantly.

"Men and women of Podmyn and those of you who have come from the outlying districts, may I begin by saying what a pleasure it is to see you all assembled here today," the officer began.

"This is very odd," Manachee whispered to Bea. "A security chief doesn't normally bother with flattery. There must be something very nasty coming up."

"I am speaking to you today on behalf of our new Leader," the man continued.

"Long live Sigmundus the Second!" shouted a group of security officers. Immediately the crowd understood what was expected of them. "Long live Sigmundus the Second!" they chorused.

"Many of you good people traveled to Ellison for the funeral of our former Leader," the officer went on, "and you will have seen with your own eyes that even while the streets were thronged with grateful citizens, many of whom had stood in line for hours to pay their respects to the founder of our nation, a handful of depraved and ruthless individuals made a despicable attempt to disrupt the ceremony."

He paused and shook his head as if the thought of such wickedness were almost too much to bear. "You may well ask how it is that crime has raised its ugly head in our society once more. You believed that this terrible sickness had been eradicated once and for all. Well, you were right. It has been. These attempts to undermine everything we have built under the benevolent guidance of Dr. Sigmundus, and everything we are hoping to build under the inspired leadership of his successor, come . . . from outside."

Bea, Albigen and Manachee looked at each other.

"For a long time our neighbors in Tavor have cast jealous eyes upon our noble country. They have looked upon our well-organized society, our prosperous citizens, our safe and pleasant streets, and they have envied us. Now their envy has boiled over, and they have sent their agents into Gehenna to undermine everything we have worked so hard to build."

"Shame on them!" shouted the security guards.

"Shame on them!" the audience echoed.

"Why is he blaming Tavor?" Bea asked herself. "Does he really not know that the smoke bombs were the work of the Púca?"

"But there is worse to come," the officer continued. "Much worse. For these treacherous agents are not content with disrupting the funeral of our former Leader. No, that was only the beginning. We have it on good authority that they want to take over our country and have been busy recruiting collaborators from within Gehenna itself. Yes, my friends, there are traitors amongst us."

There was a collective gasp as he said this.

"While our new Leader has been busy picking up the reins of

power, these vile scum have spread their contamination into every town in Gehenna. But do not fear, my friends! Sigmundus the Second knows what the people of Gehenna are made of! He knows that we are prepared to fight and to win—come what may. Am I right?"

"Yes!" they shouted back.

"Sigmundus the Second knows that he can rely upon the loyalty of the people of Gehenna. And he has given each and every one of you a unique chance to prove yourselves. Today, ladies and gentlemen, I can announce the formation of a new force in our country that will tackle the enemies of Gehenna. This force is to be called the Faithful."

Bea gasped. Hadn't her father said he would be working with the Faithful?

"At the end of our meeting today," the officer went on, "my officers will be taking the names and details of all those brave men and women, all those patriotic individuals, who want to volunteer to help save their country in its time of greatest need. I know that every one of you will want to be the first in line. But before that happens, there is something else that must be taken care of. An unpleasant duty, ladies and gentlemen, but one that I will not shirk. As I told you, there are traitors all over Gehenna. Even here in Podmyn itself. Well, it is time we showed them how we intend to repay such treachery."

He turned to his men. "You know what you have to do," he told them.

The security guards pushed their way through the bewildered onlookers, roughly elbowing aside anyone who got in their way. There was a shriek as they seized a woman from the midst of the crowd.

"Stop! You're making a mistake!" the woman cried.

"I know that voice!" Bea said to herself.

As the guards emerged from the crowd, Bea saw that their prisoner was the woman she had sat next to on the bus when she had traveled to the funeral of Dr. Sigmundus.

"I don't believe this for a moment," Bea said quietly. "She's not clever enough to be a traitor!"

"Keep your voice down!" Albigen hissed.

The guards dragged their victim over towards the corn exchange and forced her to stand on a wooden chair on the pavement outside. Meanwhile, another guard was busy on the balcony above, lowering a rope with a noose on the end.

"I can't watch this!" Bea muttered.

"Stay where you are!" Albigen whispered back.

"We know all about you," the guard told the sobbing woman, placing the noose around her neck and pulling it tight. "We've been watching your every move."

"It isn't true!" she protested. "I haven't done anything. I love my country. I would never do anything to harm—"

But she did not finish her sentence. The chair on which she was standing was kicked away beneath her.

Bea shut her eyes.

"Death to all traitors!" the security guards shouted.

This time there was no echoing cry from the crowd, only shocked silence.

The security guards left the woman hanging there. Then they crossed the square and smashed the windows of the shop in which she had worked and lived. They kicked open the door and turned everything upside down.

When the guards had finished, the officer on the wooden platform began speaking once more. "That is how we deal with traitors," he declared. "We show them no mercy because to show mercy is to show weakness. And now, ladies and gentlemen, I invite you all to do your duty to your Leader and your country. Step up to the front and sign up for the Faithful."

Crowds of people began pushing their way to the front, eager to display their loyalty lest they, too, be considered potential traitors.

"Let's get out of here," Albigen said.

"There's something I have to do first," Bea replied.

She made her way through the crowd towards the baker's shop with Albigen and Manachee following behind her. The townsfolk of Podmyn had already taken advantage of its owner's disgrace by helping themselves to the produce on the shelves.

"You're too late. There's nothing left!" an old woman with no front teeth told them.

But Bea had not come for bread. She stepped inside the front door, then quickly made her way behind the counter to the room at the back where the bread was baked. From there, a corridor led to the backyard and here, as she had expected, she found the woman's dog wagging his tail and looking expectantly at her.

He was little more than a puppy, friendly and inquisitive. Bea had no trouble convincing him that he ought to come with her. Next to the door was a leash, which she attached to his collar. Then she led him back through the house into the square, where Albigen and Manachee were waiting for her.

"What are you doing with that dog?" Albigen asked incredulously.

"He belongs to the woman who was hanged," Bea explained. "I couldn't just leave him there. She told me the neighbors didn't like him barking. They'd probably have him killed, too."

Albigen looked around anxiously. "Bea, please—we've got enough problems feeding ourselves without adding another hungry mouth."

"Let her keep him," Manachee said gently.

They both looked at him in surprise. Manachee did not often come down firmly on one side or the other.

"Well then, you're completely responsible for looking after him!" Albigen told Bea.

"Of course I am," Bea said, bending down and stroking the dog, who immediately turned his head and licked her hand with his big, sloppy tongue. "See, he already knows that."

THE DUCHESS

Nyro and Osman made their way silently along the tunnel. The right-hand fork sloped steeply downwards, but it was broad and high-ceilinged, with plenty of room for them to walk upright. Soon Nyro forgot about the Chief Justice and found himself thinking instead of the terrible fate that had befallen his friend Luther. He described what he had seen to Osman, including Luther's warning about the bridge that was being built between the Nakara and the Resurrection Fields.

A little later they rounded another bend and emerged at the other end of the tunnel. Stepping out into the light, they found themselves in a clearing beyond which stretched a dense forest. A tall, striking-looking woman dressed all in black was standing beside a crude wooden hut. She stood very upright, and the impression of height was increased by how her hair was piled on the top of her head in an elaborate coiffure. Around her neck she wore a rope of pearls, and diamonds glittered at her ears. To Nyro she looked like a duchess. However, despite this air of nobility, the woman seemed to be in distinctly reduced circumstances, for she was standing beside an open fire over which there hung a large cooking pot. From time to time she stirred the pot with a wooden spoon, and the smell that arose from it was quite delicious.

"Perhaps we can get directions from this woman," Nyro said.

"We could ask her for something to eat first," Osman suggested.

Nyro was about to protest that they had no time to waste when he realized that he was actually very hungry. After all, he had eaten nothing for twenty-four hours.

The woman nodded and smiled as they drew closer, as if she had been expecting them. "You're just in time," she announced. She gestured towards a wooden table and benches nearby. "I take it you would like some soup."

"That's very kind of you, madam," Osman said.

Beside the fire, on a large flat rock, there were three earthenware bowls into which the woman now began to ladle soup.

"We were wondering whether you had heard of the Resurrection Fields?" Nyro said when they were sitting down at the table.

"Of course, serving soup is not the sort of thing I'm used to," continued the duchess, as if she had not noticed his question at all. "When my dear husband was alive, we never kept fewer than thirty servants, you know." She sighed deeply.

"May I offer you our commiserations on your bereavement, madam," Osman said.

"Thank you, sir. You are very kind. Very kind indeed. But all the kindness in the world cannot make up for what I have lost. My husband was a truly remarkable person. A man of power and a man of vision. How seldom we find these two qualities together nowadays." She paused in her ladling, apparently lost in recollections of her late husband's virtues.

Nyro decided to try again. "We were looking for the Resurrection Fields," he said. "Do you know where we can find them?"

"We had our enemies, of course," the duchess went on, still oblivious to his inquiry. "No one who finds himself in a position of authority can avoid making enemies. There were plots and rebellions all the time. And so we had to take the necessary measures, painful though they may have been. It was for the greater good. You must see that?"

She looked eagerly at them both.

"Of course, madam," Osman said.

"Absolutely," Nyro agreed. "The Resurrection—" he began.

But she was not to be deterred. "None of them was innocent," she announced angrily, "whatever you may have heard to the contrary."

"I can assure you, madam, we have heard nothing whatsoever on this subject," Osman told her.

She frowned sternly in his direction. "Propaganda spreads like cancer," she replied. Then she seemed to relent a little. "However, I am happy to learn that you have been unaffected." She dipped the ladle into the cooking pot once more, then paused again. "There is such a thing as a necessary evil," she declared. "You understand, don't you?"

They both nodded. By now Nyro had given up the idea of asking her about the Resurrection Fields, at least until they had eaten their meal. The smell of the soup was driving him crazy.

"That is exactly what the camps were," the duchess declared.

"The camps?" Osman asked.

"Yes, the camps. A necessary evil. People had to be kept somewhere while they were waiting to be processed. We spent as much as we could afford under the circumstances. Conditions were a little difficult sometimes, but these were conspirators, assassins, terrorists. I know what you will say," she added sharply. "You will bring up the children."

"I had no intention—" Osman began, but she cut him off.

"Those children were as bad as the adults," she told him. "Worse, in many cases. We could not afford to show mercy merely on account of their age. It was a matter of survival. Theirs or ours."

The woman looked for a moment as if she might strike Osman with the ladle instead of serve him soup, but then she seemed to pull herself together. "I am forgetting the rules of hospitality," she said. "My poor husband would not have approved. You know, he used to say that whatever went on outside the walls of the palace, we should always treat our guests with courtesy."

Despite this declaration, she made no further move to serve the soup. At last, deciding that she had forgotten it altogether, Nyro got to his feet and made his way over towards the cooking pot, intent on completing the job himself.

The duchess looked appalled at this sudden act of decisiveness. "What do you think you're doing?" she demanded. "Sit down immediately!"

But it was already too late. Nyro had gone near enough to glimpse the contents of the cooking pot, and what he saw made him stop in his tracks and nearly gag. A man's head was floating on the surface of the pot, its two eyes staring glassily upwards.

"Osman!" Nyro said. "We have to go!"

Osman frowned at him. "Not before we have some soup," he said.

"Now, Osman!" Nyro said.

Osman sprang to his feet.

The woman glanced from one of them to the other. "So you are part of the conspiracy, too," she angrily declared. "I should have known!" Bending down, she pulled an iron poker from the fire. The end was glowing red-hot. "I know how to deal with conspirators!" she said. "I've had plenty of experience."

Osman began backing away as she moved towards him, holding the poker in front of her. Nyro picked up one of the soup bowls.

"Have some soup!" he shouted.

She turned, and he threw the contents in her face. "Run!" he shouted to Osman.

The two of them raced into the forest, leaving the woman screaming as she clutched at her scalded skin.

STONES

Kidu did not want to stay near the beehive huts just so that Dante could keep an eye on Bea.

"Nothing here!" he pointed out, disgustedly. "No tree but Enil's tree!" A landscape without vegetation was an atrocity in Kidu's eyes. "Nothing to eat! Nothing to drink!"

"There are muzur," Dante pointed out.

"Too few!" Kidu said angrily. "Besides, pikarakacheep everywhere. Eat muzur first."

"Pikarakacheep?"

"Ugly creatures! Covered in green scales. Crawl out from under stones. Long tongue dart out. Muzur gone. Nothing for Kidu."

"I just need to stay here for a little while longer," Dante pleaded. "It's important."

"Everything Giddim want always important."

"Please, Kidu, just a little longer."

Kidu sighed. Before sharing Kidu's body, Dante had not known that a bird could sigh, but he had soon learned that it was one of Kidu's favorite ways of expressing himself. Nevertheless, the bird did not attempt to leave, contenting himself instead with flying furiously at any lizard that dared stick its head out of a crack in the stonework.

Dante continued to turn over in his mind the message carved on the stone step. It made no sense to him, but it had to be important. Why else would his mother have wanted him to ensure that Bea discovered it?

When every other hope has fled,
When he is lost who once was found,
Climb the stairs and greet the dawn,
Make the world's most ancient sound.

The message obviously had something to do with the pillar. Someone—presumably Bea—was meant to climb the steps at dawn. But what then? He went over in his mind what he had learned of the bird's beliefs about the pillar. According to Kidu, the pillar had been built by Enil, a good and powerful human who had governed all creatures on the earth. He had built it for Iggigi, who was the mate of Anki, the god responsible for creating the universe.

Obviously Kidu's beliefs could not be taken at face value. The universe had not begun as a feather that had fallen from the wing of a giant bird. Nevertheless, there might be something in the bird's story that was important, some tiny grain of truth buried beneath the mythology built up by generations of creatures.

As Dante was thinking about this, he spied Bea coming out of her stone hut accompanied by a dog. Then a figure materialized out of thin air just behind her. Was it the same one Dante had glimpsed when he first arrived at the pillar? It was hard to tell from this distance. The dog began barking aggressively, but Bea pulled him away impatiently as if she did not realize someone was there.

Dante urged Kidu to fly closer, and the bird reluctantly agreed, landing beside the path a few yards ahead of Bea. Now that Dante could see the face of Bea's pursuer, his spirits sank. They had met before. When Dante had been taken prisoner in Tavor, he had entered the Odylic realm only to find someone waiting for him. At first he had believed he was meeting his long-lost brother—a mistake that had nearly cost him his life, for this was Set, who had once been a messenger of the Odyll but now dwelt in the depths of the Nakara, feeding upon the hopes and dreams of others.

While Dante was recalling this, Set drew level with Kidu. Then, moving as swiftly as one of the lizards that darted back and forth between the stones, he bent down and seized the bird in his right hand.

"Well, Dante Cazabon," he said with an evil grin, "fancy meeting you here. Everyone's looking for you, you know. Tzavinyah would love to know where you are. But of course he only knows what he's told. Right now he wouldn't know you if you perched on his finger and sang for him. But I have peered into places where he does not dare look. I have no trouble recognizing you—even in this ridiculous disguise."

He squeezed Kidu's body to emphasize his point, and Dante felt the bird's terror mounting so strongly that he feared Kidu's tiny heart might burst.

"Your little friend Bea interests me," Set continued. "She's so full of goodness," he said with a curl of his lip. "Dear Tzavinyah positively dotes on her. I believe he has some very important role lined up for her, now that you're not on the scene anymore. Well, it won't do him any good, because I've decided to take her in hand. I see her as a fabulous challenge. And I don't want you interfering. So I should fly away if I were you, otherwise I might have to mention the fact that you're hiding in this fragile bundle of feathers to our friend the bridge builder."

He paused, then smiled unpleasantly once more. "Oh, you don't know about the bridge yet, do you? I honestly don't understand why everyone makes such a fuss about you, Dante Cazabon. You're always two steps behind the game, aren't you?" He shook his head. "You'll find out about the bridge in due course, like everyone else. In the meantime, stay out of my way."

With that, he gave Kidu a crushing squeeze before tossing him into the air and walking away.

Kidu's wings fluttered feebly, but despite his best efforts he could not manage to stay aloft. He landed with a bone-jarring thump on the ground.

Dante felt the bird's pain as Kidu lay on the ground, breathing in shallow gasps, his heart racing, his body aching. But worse than the physical pain was the fear. Kidu had not understood everything Set had said, but the overall meaning was clear enough. Set had played with him like a cat plays with its prey before killing it, and though Kidu was still alive, he was not sure he wouldn't rather be dead and gone from a world that had such creatures in it.

Bea returned from her walk feeling just as discontented as when she began it. For days now she had felt a growing sense of frustration. She tried to inspire herself by thinking about what Tzavinyah had told her. But the memory of his hopeful words was fading from her mind, and she was finding it hard to believe he had really appeared to her. The hanging of the woman in Podmyn haunted her: the way the crowd—herself among them—had just stood there and watched. And yet what could she have done? To have tried to prevent it would only have got her arrested. It would not have saved the woman's life.

She tried to rid her mind of the picture of the woman's face just before the chair was kicked away from underneath her. But it would not disappear. And this had been carried out on the orders of her former friend! She shook her head in disbelief. She still cherished, deep within her, the belief that it wasn't really him. But, if not, then what had happened to the real Dante?

Outside the meetinghouse, Albigen, Maeve, Manachee and Seersha were waiting for her. The Púca had been monitoring events in Podmyn since the day of the hanging, and Albigen had come up with a plan to increase their diminishing supply of food. Today all those who had enlisted in the ranks of the Faithful would be leaving to begin their duties. A special train had been arranged to take them, and their supplies, from Podmyn's tiny railway station to their new headquarters up north. A farewell ceremony had been planned in the town. While the festivities were taking place, the Púca would divert some of the supplies from the train to one of their trucks. Seersha had volunteered to drive the truck; Manachee, Maeve and Bea had agreed to do the loading.

"Is everybody ready?" Albigen asked when they were all assembled.

They nodded.

"Remember, don't hurry when you're carrying the crates. Just look as if you're doing your job. And Seersha, make sure you keep the engine running."

They soon joined a string of ancient trucks and cars, battered tractors and horse-drawn carts on the road to Podmyn. People were traveling there from all the outlying areas with the intention of either boarding the special train or waving off members of their family who were joining the Faithful.

Albigen and Maeve had visited the town the night before to make their preparations. They had discovered a disused entrance at the side of the railway station. It was padlocked, but Albigen had brought along a pair of bolt cutters. This was where they parked the truck that morning, hidden from the crowds behind an abandoned railway carriage.

At the front of the railway station a band was playing patriotic music. They were a motley collection of musicians: mostly old men, with a couple of young boys playing the trumpet and bass drum and a lone girl on the clarinet. People were in a festive mood, grinning broadly at their neighbors. Those who had volunteered for the Faithful were being congratulated and having their hands shaken as they hung out of the train windows, waving cheerily to friends and relations.

Dozens of wooden crates had been delivered to the railway station, and volunteers were busily loading them onto the train. Manachee, Maeve, Bea and Albigen joined the line of loaders. First Manachee and Maeve picked up a crate and walked off with it. Then it was the turn of Bea and Albigen. Bea bent down and gripped her end. The crate was surprisingly heavy, and she staggered as she took the weight.

"They won't be short of a bite to eat!" quipped a red-faced man standing in line behind her.

Bea gave him a polite smile. The last thing she wanted to do was to get involved in a conversation with someone.

When they reached the platform, they should have turned right and made their way to the rear of the train, where the goods carriages were situated. Instead, they turned left. There were so many people milling about on the platform that no one paid them any attention as they shuffled towards the side entrance.

Ahead of them, Manachee and Maeve had already disappeared through the gate into the yard where the truck was parked. Just as it looked as if the whole operation was going to pass off smoothly, Bea heard a shout behind her. She turned and saw the red-faced man standing near the entrance, trying to attract her attention.

"Keep going!" Albigen urged. "Don't take any notice of him."

But the red-faced man was shouting now and other people were starting to pay attention.

"Tavorian spies!" someone else shouted. Immediately, the cry was taken up by others. A moment later a pair of security officers was racing down the platform towards them.

"Leave the crate!" Albigen said.

Bea dropped her end and they set off running for the side gate. But a glimpse over her shoulder revealed that one of the security guards was right behind them. She followed Albigen through the gate and tore across the yard to where Maeve and Manachee were leaning out of the rear doors of the truck, urging them on.

Albigen leapt into the truck and turned to shout encouragement to Bea, but at that moment she felt the security guard grabbing her arm. She struggled to shake him off but he had hold of her now, and his colleague was already making his way through the gate into the yard.

Albigen jumped down from the truck, picked up a length of wood that was lying on the ground nearby and raced towards Bea. The security guard saw him coming and let go of Bea, reaching for the baton he wore at his side. But Albigen was too quick for him. He brought the length of wood down so hard on the man's arm that Bea was convinced she heard the bone break. Then, as his opponent bent over in pain, Albigen hurled the length of wood in the direction of the second security guard. He dodged it easily but it was enough to slow him down.

"Come on!" Albigen shouted. The two of them scrambled into the truck, and Seersha immediately raced off while her passengers struggled to avoid being flung out of the still-open doors.

Nobody said very much on the way home. Plenty of people had had the opportunity to get a good look at their van, as well as at them, and the townsfolk would be on their guard from now on. All chance of visiting Podmyn again had been lost.

"We're losing our touch," Albigen said sadly.

When they got back to the beehive huts, the rest of the Púca were waiting eagerly, and hearing the attempts of their friends to look on the bright side only made the disappointment greater.

"At least you didn't come back empty-handed," said Keeva, Maeve's mother.

"It might have been better if we had," Bea replied.

But Keeva was not the kind of person to be easily discouraged. "Let's get the crate open and see what we've got," she said.

It wasn't easy to open the crate. The lid had been firmly nailed down, but Manachee eventually pried it up with the help of a crowbar. He pushed aside a layer of straw and then gasped.

"What is it?" Bea asked.

"See for yourselves."

Bea and Albigen bent over the crate and examined its contents. It was filled with stones. There was nothing else. No wonder it had been so heavy!

Albigen swore and kicked the side of the crate. "It doesn't make sense," he said. "What the hell are they playing at?"

"Maybe somebody made a mistake?" Keeva suggested.

Suddenly Bea understood. "This was no mistake," she said. "They're not planning to feed these volunteers."

"Why not?"

"Because they won't last long enough," she said. "They're volunteering for an early death. And my father is going to be in charge of the process."

THE FOREST OF SECRET FEARS

The forest into which Nyro had run after glimpsing the severed head seemed to belong to the deepest memory of the world. The trees were ancient and huge, their thick black trunks covered with moss and lichen. The ground was carpeted with layer upon layer of rotting leaves, and the air was heavy with the perfume of decay.

It was not a welcoming place, yet it was strangely familiar, and as Nyro blundered through the trees he found himself thinking, "I've been here before. But when?"

Of course! He had visited this wood in his sleep, for this was the place where nightmares were born, where they grew secretly in the darkness—deformed, waiting for their chance to enter the minds of men, women and, best of all, children.

He should never have come here, but in his shock, Nyro had just plunged headlong in among the trees, forgetting about everything else. Even Osman!

He stopped and called out Osman's name, but the forest swallowed up his voice so that he sounded like a little lost child crying for his mother. He looked around for the way out, but the trees were identical in all directions. Somewhere behind him he thought he heard a mocking laugh. He swiveled round, but there was no one there.

Elsewhere Osman was busy trying to recognize the smell in the forest. It did not smell like a wood at all, in his opinion. It seemed like more of an indoor smell—artificial, sterile, clinical. Of course! It smelled like a hospital.

It seemed to be getting stronger all the time, a cocktail of different odors. On the surface was a clean fragrance, reminding him of medicine, disinfectant and air freshener. But below that was the odor of sickness, the insistent perfume of disease.

Osman knew exactly when and where he had smelled this before. He had been a young man, sitting beside a hospital bed. In the bed was his father, though illness and pain had made him barely recognizable. Once, he had been strong and full of vigor, but death was devouring him bit by bit, reducing him to a husk. Osman had not wanted to witness this, but it had been expected of him, and so he had sat on the chair while the minutes ticked by and the air grew thick with pain.

"That is what will happen to you," said a voice in his ear.

Osman turned to see who had spoken, but there was no one there. Instead, where there had been trees, there was now a hospital bed and on the bed was a shriveled figure. Himself.

"You will inherit your father's disease, just as you have inherited everything else of his," the voice continued.

Osman nodded. He had only to look in a mirror to see that he now looked exactly as his father had at his age. As he had taken on his father's features, so he would take on his illness.

"No medicine exists that will help you," the voice told him. "You will beg for the end to come, but it will not increase its pace. Death will creep towards you. It will relish your suffering."

"Why are you telling me this?" Osman demanded.

"For your own good, of course," the voice answered silkily.

"What do you mean?"

"It doesn't have to be like this." The voice was reassuring now, friendly and comforting. "There is another way."

"What is the other way?"

"Make death come to you."

"What do you mean?"

"You know what I mean."

* * *

Nyro heard movement and glimpsed a shadowy form among the trees up ahead. "Is that you, Osman?" he called out, trying to sound confident.

A huge creature lumbered out of the trees towards him. Dressed in a long shapeless garment made of what looked like sackcloth, it was shaped like a man but very much bigger. Its arms were far too long for its body, reaching down as far as its knees. In one hand the creature grasped a long knife with a wicked-looking blade. But Nyro scarcely even glanced at any of this, for his gaze was fixed on the creature's face. Where a man would have eye sockets, this creature's face was completely smooth. It advanced towards him slowly, swinging its arms at its sides and sniffing the air with a series of snuffling grunts.

Nyro wanted to turn and run but he was rooted to the spot.

"You cannot run from me," the creature said, in a deep, booming voice. "I will always find you by the smell of your fear."

"I'm not afraid of you," Nyro replied.

The creature's laugh seemed to fill the forest. "Everyone is afraid of me," it told him, "for I am Fear itself." It held up the knife, the blade of which was as long as Nyro's arm. "There is nothing that my knife cannot cut. Alive or dead."

Nyro took a careful step backwards. Immediately

the creature thrust the knife forward until its point was barely an inch from his chest.

"I wouldn't do that," it told him. "You see, I know what you are thinking before you even think it. Right now, for example, you're thinking that there will be no way out of this forest, that you are trapped in here forever. Aren't you?"

Nyro made no reply.

"And you're right," the creature went on. "You *are* trapped here forever. Even if you could find a way out, you can never get back to your own world. This is where your ridiculous little journey finishes."

The creature's words felt like a huge weight around Nyro's neck, but he struggled against his despair. He had to get out of here, whatever the creature said. What was it Luther had warned him about? There was someone who had to be stopped.

"You are thinking of what your friend Luther told you," the creature declared. "But why listen to him? Look at what he has become—a voice that speaks from the heart of a thorn tree. Rooted in stony ground, buffeted by the wind, trapped for eternity. Pay no heed to Luther's ridiculous words. He cannot help you and you cannot help him."

But something deep within Nyro refused to accept this. "No doubt you're right," he conceded. "But even so, I might just as well go on trying to find my way out of here as give up."

A low, rumbling growl came from the creature's throat. "There *is* no way out of here," it insisted.

Strangely enough, the creature's growl had quite the opposite effect on Nyro from what was intended. He realized that he at least had the power to annoy the creature. "Why are you so anxious to persuade me to give up?" he asked.

"I only wish to save you a great deal of trouble," the creature replied, in its most reasonable voice.

"No, you don't," Nyro thought. "You just want to make me miserable, because you feed off other people's misery." The creature was nearly twice as tall as Nyro and brandishing its knife right in front of him, but Nyro was beginning to grasp the key to defeating it. It could not see him; it could only smell his fear. And though it could sense some of his thoughts, Nyro suspected that they were only the negative ones.

He began, quite deliberately, to think about a summer, three years earlier, when his parents had taken him on vacation to a small seaside town. When they had arrived at their destination, instead of driving straight to their lodgings, they had gone first to look at the sea, parking the car and walking over the sand dunes. Nyro would never forget the moment they reached the top of the last dune and the sea spread out before them, with the sinking sun creating a golden avenue that led all the way to the horizon.

As he thought about this, he stepped away from the eyeless creature's knife.

"Where are you?" the creature demanded.

Nyro smiled but said nothing.

"You can't escape!" the creature warned.

Nyro continued to move noiselessly away.

The creature slashed furiously through the air, but it came nowhere near Nyro.

"I will tear you into little pieces!" the creature roared, and it flung its weapon in what it hoped was Nyro's direction. But the knife lodged harmlessly in a nearby tree. Carefully Nyro pulled it free. Then he walked calmly away, still holding the knife and thinking of his vacation by the sea, remembering how it had felt to plunge into the water in the morning: freezing cold but absolutely wonderful. Life was worth living, he reminded himself, and he was going to do everything in his power to find his way back to a world where you could run into the sea and laugh out loud with the pure joy of it.

It didn't take him long to find Osman. His friend was standing, staring into space, with a look of complete despair.

"What are you thinking?" Nyro asked him.

"I was trying to decide how I should kill myself," Osman told him, glancing at the knife. "It is not easy in a place like this. There are so few options."

"You can't kill yourself," Nyro told him. "We've got work to do."

"Work?"

"We have to stop that bridge from being built."

"But we don't even know where it is."

"True," Nyro agreed. "But I'm going to find it and you're going to help me."

"Do you really think we can do that?"

Nyro smiled, remembering how he had put this same question to Osman when Osman had first suggested finding Luther. It seemed a long time ago now. "Yes, I do," he said. "Of course, it will be dangerous, and difficult and frightening. But worth doing. And that's what counts, don't you think?"

Osman thought about this. Then he, too, smiled. "You're absolutely right," he said.

THE GREAT FLOCK

The Púca were gathered in the meetinghouse, discussing the results of the failed raid on Podmyn. Everyone accepted that the mission had been a disaster, but no one could agree what their next move should be. Bea listened to her friends' suggestions with growing impatience. None of them even knew what they wanted to achieve. Only Seersha and Malachy seemed undaunted.

"We have to hold on to hope," Seersha said. "Malachy and I believed we had lost each other for good, but now we're back together again. That was made possible by two things: our longing to be free and the inspiration of others who were determined not to give up."

This little speech did something to rally people's spirits. A while later Maeve and Keeva returned from scouting out Duran, a town to the northeast of Podmyn. People greeted them enthusiastically, eager for some positive news. "There's been another special broadcast," Maeve announced. "Apparently some sort of revolution has been taking place in Tavor. According to the broadcast, troops led by someone called Brigadier Giddings have surrounded the government buildings there and arrested the leaders. Giddings has declared himself the new ruler and pledged his friendship to Sigmundus the Second."

"Are the people of Tavor going to let that happen?" Albigen asked.

"There's fighting on the streets," Maeve said. "But according to the broadcast, the resistance is weak."

"They would say that!"

"More people are being urged to sign up for the Faithful," Keeva told them. "There's a train leaving from Duran tomorrow."

That was when Bea made up her mind. "I'm going to be on it," she announced.

The others turned and looked at her in astonishment.

"What do you mean?" Albigen demanded.

"Just what I say," Bea replied. "I'm volunteering for the Faithful."

Everyone immediately began arguing with her, but Bea refused to discuss it further. Instead, she drew Seersha aside. "I want you to promise to look after the dog for me," she said. "I haven't even given him a name yet, poor thing. But I've got a feeling about him, as if he might have some important part to play in all this."

Seersha searched her friend's face. "Of course I will. But I don't understand who you are these days, Bea," she said.

Bea gave a wry smile. "I'm not sure I understand that myself," she replied. "I just know this is what I have to do."

It had taken Kidu several days to recover from his encounter with Set, days during which he perched listlessly on the steps of the stone pillar, muttering to himself about the unfairness of his life. Often Dante had to prompt him to eat but even these gentle reminders only served to plunge Kidu deeper into depression.

"Oh yes," he said gloomily. "Giddim look after Kidu. Giddim take good care of Kidu. Don't worry, Kidu, you will not be trapped, he say. No one interested in you. Then what happen? Kidu get squeezed and squeezed and squeezed until bones almost break. But who cares? Not Giddim. Much more interested in watching female zittenziteen. Please stay, Kidu, he say, even though Evil One say no, don't watch, fly away. Still Giddim keep watching, and very soon Evil One come back. Then he say you were warned but you not listen. This time I squeeze harder. Break all Kidu's bones. What then, Giddim? Eh? What then?"

Dante had given up arguing with Kidu. He was too busy trying to understand the meaning of the message Bea had uncovered and trying to think of a way to communicate with her, though the chances of Kidu ever going anywhere near her again were extremely remote. "If only I could enter the Odylic realm," Dante thought, but he knew that the moment he tried to do so, he would find Orobas waiting.

As he was pondering all this, the Púca began streaming out of the meetinghouse. Most of them made their way back to their stone huts, but Bea and Albigen continued walking towards the pillar. It soon became clear that they were arguing fiercely.

"The whole idea is madness!" Albigen was saying. "You will be walking into the heart of evil without any idea of what you will do when you get there. What do you think will happen?"

"I don't know," Bea admitted.

"Then I'll tell you what will happen," Albigen went on. "They will catch you and then they will do terrible things to you. I know what they are like."

"So do I. But I have to try," Bea replied.

Albigen seized her by the shoulders and looked her right in the eyes. "Please, you must listen to me, Bea," he said. "There are things that are worse than death, much worse! And it's not just your own safety you need to think about. You'll tell them everything and then we'll all be finished."

Dante listened with growing alarm. What was Bea planning to do?

"I'm sorry, Albigen," Bea said. She reached up and gently took his hands from her shoulders. "I know it sounds crazy, and you're right, I'm putting everyone at risk. But remember what Ezekiel always told us: everything that can possibly happen always does. It's just that we only choose to believe in some of those possibilities. Well, I'm choosing to believe that this is what I was meant to do and that it will work out for the best, and I need you to have faith in me."

Albigen shook his head. "Ezekiel had faith," he pointed out. "Now he lies under a pile of stones. I don't want that to happen to you, Bea."

"Ezekiel played his part and I'm going to play mine," Bea said, and with that she turned and walked rapidly away.

Dante was about to ask Kidu to follow when he realized that something very unusual was happening to the bird. Kidu was no longer listless and apathetic. Instead, his whole body was alert, and he seemed to be listening. Deliberately Dante lowered the barrier he had built between his own mind and Kidu's. He allowed himself to share the bird's thoughts fully.

It was as though a musical note was sounding in the bird's mind, a note that was full of a wild longing. The note was only faint as yet, but it was growing stronger all the time—and the more Kidu listened to it, the more excited he became.

"What is it, Kidu?" Dante demanded.

"Satsumballa," Kidu answered.

"What does that mean?"

But Kidu did not even bother to reply. Forgetting his injuries, he spread his wings and took to the air.

"Wait, Kidu!" Dante protested. "I need to stay by Enil's tree."

"Satsumballa!" Kidu insisted.

The bird's mind was filled with that strange musical sound, which was changing now, moving up and down the scale, weaving a kind of ecstatic melody so that even Dante understood how thrilling it was. But what did it mean?

Soon he saw a number of black specks in the distance—birds

flying in the same direction as Kidu. Others appeared, coming from a different part of the sky, then more still. Before very long Kidu was surrounded by birds, each one occupying its own space, yet all coordinating their flight by some mysterious process, so that when the wing tips of one bird tilted slightly, the wing tips of all tilted in exactly the same way.

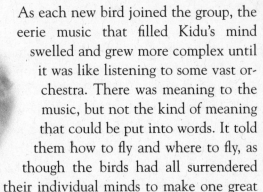

As each new bird joined the group, the eerie music that filled Kidu's mind swelled and grew more complex until it was like listening to some vast orchestra. There was meaning to the music, but not the kind of meaning that could be put into words. It told them how to fly and where to fly, as though the birds had all surrendered their individual minds to make one great mind that was directing the behavior of them all.

"So this is what it is like to be part of a flock!" Dante thought. But then he corrected himself: not *part* of a flock, for there was no room for individuality. There was just the flock. Dante could not communicate with Kidu any longer, for Kidu had shut down his distinct personality to make room for the collective identity.

Now the music began to change, and Dante saw that other flocks made up of other species were coming from other parts of the sky: tiny songbirds and great strong birds of prey among them. Each species contributed its own music. But all merged together into the one. Past enmities and disputes were forgotten, generations of conflict and competition put aside as predator and prey fell into line, one behind the other.

Now Dante understood what Kidu had said before taking to the air so suddenly: satsumballa—the Great Flock. This was a once-in-a-lifetime occasion, once in many lifetimes. To the birds that filled the air all around him, the satsumballa would have been only a legend, told to them as they huddled sleepily in the nest. And now they were joining together to bring it about because an impulse had come from somewhere deep within their minds. They did not know how or where this call had originated, only that it had to be answered. So they had taken to the air without question, their excitement and certainty growing stronger with each wing beat. They did not yet know their destination, but they would recognize it when they arrived.

To human beings watching from below, it must have seemed as though an enormous black cloud made up of a million tiny particles was passing overhead. Did they realize that something as significant in human terms as a revolution or a war was taking place? No. They probably imagined it had something to do with the weather and just shook their heads and went back to their work.

By late evening the flocking was complete, and the eyes of every bird turned downwards, towards a mountain in the center of the country. Even with his lack of education, Dante had heard of this great eminence, the highest spot in all Gehenna, Mount Sulyaman.

The flock began its descent, using currents of wind to glide gracefully down in a series of spirals, instinctively coordinating their movements so that no two birds sought out the same spot and finally settling on the great shoulders of the giant rock like a covering of snow. Once more the music changed, becoming urgent and expectant as if an audience were preparing itself for a speech by some great orator.

Every nook and cranny of the mountain was covered with birds by now, and every one of them was in perfect communication with its fellows. Suddenly Dante understood what they had all come together to discuss. Him.

"Silence!"

The command echoed across the mountain as every bird ordered its fellows to be quiet.

At the very top of the mountain perched a trio of ancient buzzards. The one in the middle seemed to be the oldest of the three, perhaps the oldest bird of all. One of his eyes was missing, but there was enough cruelty in the remaining eye to make up for it. He surveyed the ranks of other birds with contempt.

"Let the Giddim Carrier come forth!" he declared.

Every bird on the mountain turned its head to look directly at Kidu. Nervously he flew up and perched on a rock in front of the buzzards.

"What have you to say for yourself?"

Kidu began to stammer out some sort of response. He told the Chief Buzzard that he had not invited the giddim to share his body, but that it had come all the same, that he had tried to make it leave him but that he had no control over it.

"Enough!" the Chief Buzzard interrupted. "A sick zimbir carries death to his nest. Everyone here knows that."

Up and down the mountain, heads nodded and the words were repeated by a million beaks.

"Giddim promise him leave soon," Kidu assured his inquisitor.

"A giddim is a false creature and not to be believed," the bird perched to the right of the Chief Buzzard said dismissively.

The Chief Buzzard ignored this intervention. He addressed himself to the assembled birds. "You all know why this has happened," he declared, "and you know what it means. Shurruppak has returned to the world."

"Shurruppak!" A horrified whisper spread through the feathered ranks.

"With every day he grows stronger," the Chief Buzzard continued. "If he is not stopped, he will devour the world. Then there will be nowhere left for the zimbir to build their nests, and an-nalugu will be lost to us."

"Annalugu will be lost!" the birds cried despairingly.

"There can be no doubt what this giddim is doing here," the Chief Buzzard went on. "It is Shurruppak's spy."

"Shurruppak's spy!" Their despair turned to anger.

"Tell them it isn't true!" Dante urged.

"Giddim not like Shurruppak," Kidu protested. "Giddim help zimbir defeat Shurruppak."

The Chief Buzzard's one eye narrowed. "You are telling me that the giddim that has taken possession of your body will help us defeat Shurruppak?" he demanded.

"Yes. Giddim strong. Giddim powerful. Giddim help zimbir. Make Shurruppak go away. Go forever."

"And how exactly will the giddim achieve this?" the Chief Buzzard asked.

"Kidu not know," Kidu admitted in a voice that was barely audible.

The Chief Buzzard nodded. "Just as I thought," he declared. "The satsumballa has reached its verdict. Death!"

Malachy, who had spent years working in the civil service, had no difficulty preparing a set of false identification papers for Bea. Seersha cut her friend's hair short, just in case there might be anyone in Duran who had witnessed the raid in Podmyn. There were tears in the old woman's eyes as the locks of hair tumbled to the ground. Albigen watched the proceedings in silence, but his grim expression spoke volumes.

Every one of them had tried to persuade Bea to change her mind, but their efforts only made her more adamant. "Look for the hardest choice," Tzavinyah had told her.

When Albigen drove her to Duran the next morning, Maeve and Seersha insisted on coming along, too, to see her off. Albigen stopped the truck on the outskirts and they all got out. First Maeve hugged Bea, then Seersha followed suit. Seersha's hug was so tight Bea could hardly breathe. Finally it was Albigen's turn.

"It's not too late to change your mind, Bea," he said.

"I know what I'm doing."

He sighed. "Perhaps, and perhaps not . . ."

"Well, we'll soon find out," Bea said as brightly as she could.

The others nodded. Maeve and Seersha got back into the truck, but Albigen hesitated. "Bea," he said, "I know that you and Dante were . . ." Then he stopped.

"What?" Bea asked.

Albigen shook his head. "It doesn't matter. Good luck." He leaned forward and kissed her lightly on the cheek; then he, too, got back in the truck and started up the engine. Bea watched while the truck turned around, then left.

As she set off on the last mile towards Duran, Bea asked herself what Albigen had been about to say before he had changed his mind. "I know that you and Dante were . . . ," he had begun. But what exactly had she and Dante been? Friends? Yes, of course they had been friends. But hadn't they been more than that? Hadn't they meant something special to each other? Bea liked to think so.

Perhaps Albigen had been about to tell her that she meant something special to him, too. That thought made her sad, for though she liked and admired Albigen, she would never feel that way about him.

But she had made up her mind to join the Faithful. Who could tell what that decision would lead to? She might never see Albigen again, or any of the others. On the other hand, she might return to them in triumph, having defeated their enemy.

Duran was a bigger town than Podmyn, and there were even more volunteers and well-wishers crowding the railway station. Plenty of people were signing up that morning. Bea joined a line and showed the enlisting officer her papers. He wrote down her details without even glancing at her face. She made her way onto the train and was lucky enough to find one of the few remaining empty seats. Those who came after her were forced to stand. When the train was finally so packed that it could not take even one more passenger, it set out on the journey north.

Despite the overcrowding, the atmosphere was festive. Farther up the carriage a group of volunteers began singing. It was a song Bea remembered her mother singing years ago, about leaving your friends behind but keeping their memory alive, lyrics that had once struck her as trite and sentimental but that now seemed almost unbearably poignant.

It was clear that her fellow passengers were looking forward to what awaited them. "We're going to show those Tavorians a thing or two," a middle-aged man with enormous ears told Bea.

"I thought the Tavorians had joined forces with us," Bea said.

"Some of them have," the man replied. "But not the diehards. They want to keep their rotten society with its crime and disorder. They'd like to infect us with it, too. They're the ones we'll be dealing with. But don't you worry"—here he tapped his nose with his finger—"we'll soon sort them out. Sigmundus the Second knows what he's doing. That's why he was picked, see? He's the man for the job. And we're the ones to back him up." He looked around the carriage with a satisfied smile as he said this, and several people grinned back at him enthusiastically.

It was an old train, and it lumbered ponderously along the tracks, often slowing down almost to a walking pace. As the journey dragged on, the mood on board began to change. Outside, the bright sunshine of the morning had turned to an overcast sky from which rain now began to slant down across the countryside. Many of the volunteers had brought nothing to eat or drink, assuming that they would be provided with food on the journey. Bea shared the sandwiches that Seersha had made for her with the man with the enormous ears. Others were not so fortunate. Gradually the atmosphere grew more somber. One or two people said that it was not right. The train should stop to let people get out and stretch their legs. Someone ought to come around handing out food. But others assured the complainers that it was obviously a mistake and would certainly be rectified when they reached their destination.

As they traveled farther north, farmland gave way to moorland. Here and there Bea glimpsed rusting machinery and great heaps of rock, like man-made hills. They were approaching the Ichor Belt, where the entire countryside had been turned over to the production of the drug on which Gehenna depended.

At seven o'clock in the evening the train reached its destination, a bleak and windswept station in the middle of nowhere. If any of the volunteers had expected a reception to match their send-off, they were sorely disappointed. There were no cheering crowds, just a line of grim-faced security guards with wooden batons hanging at their sides.

As the passengers began to file warily off the train, the officer in charge shouted at them to hurry up. Bea's fellow traveler, the man with the enormous ears, walked over to him.

"You don't understand," he began. "These people have had nothing to eat or drink since they set out. I realize that this was probably just an oversight on someone's—"

That was as far as he got. The officer brought his baton down on the man's shoulder, and he fell to the ground with a cry of pain. Bea tried to run to him, but her way was blocked by a line of security guards.

The officer looked at the rest of the volunteers. "Now you know what to expect if you step out of line!" he barked.

They were marched out of the station and along a newly laid road that cut across the countryside like a scar. After half an hour, during which some volunteers stumbled and had to be pulled to their feet by their companions, they reached their destination—a series of featureless gray buildings surrounded by a fence.

Once they had passed inside the fence, they were made to halt. Then the men and women were separated and led off to wooden huts filled with mattresses. There was still no mention of food, but by now the volunteers knew better than to complain. They lay down in their clothes on the mattresses and slept. Bea remained awake longer than most, listening to the wind shaking the thin wooden walls of their dormitory and wondering whether Albigen hadn't been right, after all, and she had made a terrible mistake. But eventually she, too, surrendered to the oblivion of sleep.

The next morning she was woken by shouting. Two burly female guards were going round the dormitory, yelling at anyone who did not stand by her bed and using their batons to prod those who were too slow.

The volunteers were given only a few minutes to put on their shoes. Then they were led out of the dormitory across the bare yard to another, larger hut, where they lined up to receive bowls of thin porridge ladled out from a huge black pot. They looked stunned as they ate in silence under the watchful eyes of their guards. There was no doubt that when they set out they had expected to find military discipline waiting for them, but none of them had imagined they would be treated like prisoners.

After the meal was over, they were led to a much larger building. Unlike the wooden huts in which they had slept and eaten, this was made of bricks and mortar and seemed to be some kind of medical center. A white-coated orderly met them inside the entrance hall and led the way to a large waiting room, where they sat on wooden chairs. They were to undergo a series of blood tests, the orderly assured them. The tests would not hurt and would be over very quickly.

One by one they were called away to a consulting room. Bea was seated near the front, so she did not have to wait long for her turn. The orderly led her down a corridor, knocked on the consulting room door and waited.

"Come in," called a voice from inside.

The orderly opened the door and pushed her forward. A middle-aged doctor was standing next to a filing cabinet. He had his back to her, but now he closed the drawer and turned around.

It was her father.

A look of horror came over his face. Then he dropped a file on the floor, bent down and picked it up. When he stood up again, the look had vanished. "Otto," he said to the orderly, "I believe I may

122

have left my other glasses in the staff room. I wonder if you wouldn't mind checking for me? My jacket is hanging on the third peg from the left. They should be in the top pocket."

The orderly nodded and left the room.

"Bea!" her father said as soon as they were alone. "What on earth are you doing here?"

"I'm a volunteer," she told him calmly.

"But this is terrible! You must leave this place immediately."

"Why? What happens here?"

Her father shook his head. "I can't tell you that."

Bea shrugged. "Then I'll stay here until I find out."

Her father ran his hand through his hair, and Bea saw for the first time that he was beginning to go thin on top. She found herself touched with pity for him. "You were always so stubborn!" he said, his voice tight with anger and exasperation. "The orderly will be back in a moment. Roll up your sleeve and listen."

Bea did as she was told, and he began the process of taking a blood sample. While he worked, he talked.

"This afternoon you will be given a new drug that is being developed here," he told her. "It is given to all new recruits. That is why the Faithful was created. To test it out."

"What is this drug?" Bea asked.

"It's called Ekktor," her father explained. "It is supposed to be an improved version of Ichor. But that's not true. I don't really understand its purpose at all. Nobody does. All I know is this: those on whom it is used do not survive long, and while they live, they are in agony."

As he said this, the door opened and the orderly returned.

THE HIDDEN PATH

"Wait!" Kidu called as the birds prepared to carry out the sentence of death. "Kidu tell zimbir great secret."

The Chief Buzzard shook his wings irritably. "Very well," he said. "We're waiting. What is this great secret of which you speak?"

"Giddim show satsumballa Hidden Path," Kidu told them.

There was a collective gasp as Kidu's words were relayed to every bird.

"No, Kidu," Dante protested inside the bird's mind. "I can't do this."

"Then Kidu and Giddim die," Kidu thought back.

"Do you take us for fools?" the Chief Buzzard snarled.

"Kidu take no one for fools. Kidu offer greatest respect. Only tell truth. Giddim show satsumballa Hidden Path."

How could Dante bring a million birds with him into the Odylic realm? It was completely impossible. And even if he succeeded, Orobas would be waiting. "I can't do this, Kidu," he repeated.

"You're asking us to believe that the giddim that possesses you has the power to show us the Hidden Path, the path that Anki herself decreed we may only find after we have first flown the thousand paths of the air?" the Chief Buzzard asked.

Kidu nodded. "Giddim can do this."

"It's a trick to enable him to escape," observed the bird to the left of the Chief Buzzard. He was the smallest of the trio of buzzards, with very pale breast feathers. Dante sensed that this was a bird who would one day challenge the Chief Buzzard for leadership. "The giddim is the offspring of Shurruppak," the pale buzzard continued. "Shurruppak's greatest wish is to devour all things, including the Hidden Path."

The Chief Buzzard listened but said nothing.

"How, then, can the giddim possibly show us the Hidden Path?" the pale buzzard demanded.

Now the buzzard on the other side spoke. "Might it be entertaining to see what the accused has in mind? What have we got to lose, after all?"

The second speaker was almost as old as the Chief Buzzard himself, and it was clear from his voice that he resented his younger companion.

Kidu nodded enthusiastically. "If giddim not show zimbir Hidden Path, let zimbir peck Kidu to death," he suggested. "But if giddim do show Hidden Path, let Kidu go free. Yes?"

All eyes were trained on the Chief Buzzard now, and for the first time since they had arrived on the mountain, Dante noticed a look of uncertainty in his solitary, bloodshot eye. At last he spoke. "For a zimbir to pretend that he can find the Hidden Path before Anki has summoned him is blasphemy."

"Blasphemy!" whispered the other birds.

"The punishment for blasphemy is death," the pale buzzard interjected with such eagerness that he was unable to stop himself hopping from foot to foot as he spoke.

The Chief Buzzard turned and gave him a withering look. "As I was saying," he continued, "to make such an assertion is blasphemy unless, of course, it happens to be true."

"Unless it happens to be true," whispered all the birds excitedly.

"How could it be true?" demanded the pale buzzard angrily.

The Chief Buzzard's eye narrowed. "I did not say it *was* true," he pointed out. "Nevertheless, everyone here has heard of the Zimbir That Is Not Zimbir."

"This is not him!" the pale buzzard cried angrily.

The Chief Buzzard drew himself up to his full height. "Do you challenge me?" he demanded.

The pale buzzard hesitated. Then he bowed his head. "I do not challenge you," he muttered.

"I thought not," said the Chief Buzzard, his one eye gleaming with triumph. He turned back to Kidu. "So, zimbir of the Kekkaka tribe," he announced, "let us see what your giddim can really do. And no tricks, or I will tear out your insides myself. And I will do it so slowly you will wish that Shurruppak himself had devoured you. Do you understand?"

"Kidu understand."

"Very well, then. Tell your giddim to begin."

"You hear him, Giddim," Kidu urged Dante silently. "Kidu done his best. Now your turn."

Kidu was asking Dante to perform a miracle. There was no other word for it. He had only been able to show Kidu the world of the Odyll because their minds were linked together and they could understand each other's thoughts. Making the same thing happen for as many birds as could cover a mountaintop was a different matter entirely. It was simply not possible. And yet … .

He recalled the strange music that had filled Kidu's mind earlier, the way that it had seemed to come from all the birds at the same time, the way they had flocked together, each one barely a wing's breadth away from its fellow but never getting in each other's way. They had all dipped their wings together, all turned in the air together and all descended onto the mountain together.

They had been of one mind!

"Where does the music of the flock come from, Kidu?" he asked.

Kidu did not respond at first, and Dante was about to ask the question again when he felt something change within Kidu's mind, as if a barrier had come down. Instead of hearing the voice of Kidu, he found that he could see Kidu's thoughts directly, as they appeared to Kidu.

At this deeper level of his mind, Kidu did not think in words, only in pictures. At first there was a tumult of images that moved too fast for Dante to grasp: clouds and lightning, the branches of a tree, a cat thrusting out its paw, a nest crowded with chicks all demanding to be fed. But then all of these gave way and in the center of Kidu's mind was a picture of a bird with its wings outstretched. The bird was shining as if it were made of light itself, and Dante knew right away that this was an image of Anki, the first bird, from whom all things had sprung.

As the image grew stronger, Dante began to hear Anki's music. It began as the sound of a bird singing in a hidden garden, a place where there were no predators, no humans, no threats of any kind. But soon it became a celebration of the world of flight, the glory of the wind, its playfulness and its power, the secrets of the paths of the air.

Dante was so completely drawn into the song he failed to notice at first that he was no longer listening to a single strand of music. Other voices had joined the chorus. Or perhaps they had been there all the time, waiting for him to sink deep enough to hear them. Dozens, hundreds, thousands of voices. At last he knew that he had reached the point where Kidu's mind was joined to the mind of the Great Flock. But could Dante connect the Great Flock to the world of the Odyll? And if he did, would he find Orobas waiting for him?

He had to keep focusing on the image of the shining bird with one part of his mind, to keep listening to the music of Anki's song, but with another part of himself he began to summon up the gray door into the Odyll. It was like trying to speak two languages at the same time, like being simultaneously asleep and awake. But that was exactly how he had first learned to enter the Odylic realm. So it was not impossible! Ezekiel Semiramis had often told him, "It is not the difficulty of the task that prevents you from succeeding. It is that you keep thinking of the difficulty. Don't think. Just do!"

The door to the Odylic realm stood open. Still listening to the music of the Great Flock, Dante stepped over the threshold. All around whirled great banks of living clouds, which changed and transformed themselves as the energy of the Odyll flowed through them. In their midst was a tunnel, shining with the same light that had flowed from the image of Anki. He was looking at the Hidden Path, and he knew exactly where it would lead: to the place he had visualized when he had begun to listen to the music of the Great Flock, the secret garden where there were no hunters, where the wind was never cruel and there was always food to eat. It was not somewhere that human beings belonged. Nevertheless, a great yearning arose within him to set out upon that path and find that garden. He knew that if he did so, he could never turn back, never reclaim his humanity. He would leave his friends behind, and they would have to sort out their own problems by themselves. But that no longer troubled him. Everything else had vanished except his desire to follow the Hidden Path.

All around him he felt the Great Flock waiting for him to lead the way, their expectation as urgent as a great river about to burst through a dam, their music swelling to fill his whole being. And he knew that he was going to do it! He would lead them to the world they had been promised. Because he was the one who had been chosen. He was the Zimbir That Is Not Zimbir.

THE BRIDGE OF SOULS

At lunchtime the volunteers were given soup and bread, followed by a mug of black tea, then put to work building more huts like the ones in which they had slept. Security guards stood watching them the whole time, making sure that no one slacked even for a moment. There was no more talk about tracking down Tavorian spies. It was obvious to everyone that they were little more than slaves.

They grumbled as they worked, but no one protested out loud. The memory of the man who had been bludgeoned to the ground with a baton was still fresh in their minds. Only Bea knew that a much worse fate awaited them. She considered trying to organize some sort of breakout. But the guards all carried guns as well as batons.

As the day wore on, individual volunteers' names were called at regular intervals and they were led away. There was no explanation of where they were going, and those who were left behind muttered nervously, dreading their own summons. Bea was unloading sacks of sand from the back of a truck when her turn came. She jumped down from the truck and followed the young, shavenheaded security guard back to the building in which her father had been conducting the blood tests earlier that morning.

She was led past her father's office and up a flight of stairs. At the end of the corridor was a set of double doors. Above them was a sign that read, "No entry to unauthorized personnel." The security guard rang a bell.

As they stood waiting for the door to be opened, Bea began to notice an odd smell. It was only faint but it was disturbing:

somehow attractive and sickly at the same time. Clearly, the security guard liked it no more than she did, for he took a handkerchief from his pocket and held it over his nose and mouth.

A moment later the doors opened, and a nurse stepped out, wearing a face mask. The security guard turned gratefully away as Bea was ushered into a long room with rows of beds on either side. Many of the beds were already filled by her fellow volunteers, who lay on their backs with their eyes closed. Each one of them was attached to a drip filled with a bright purple liquid. The smell was very much stronger in here, so strong in fact that Bea gagged.

"It's just an initial reaction," the nurse said, her voice muffled by the mask. "It will pass. Now come this way, please."

She told Bea to take her shoes off, lie on one of the empty beds and roll up her sleeve.

Briefly Bea considered trying to make a break for it, but the fumes of the purple liquid seemed to be melting her resistance. "What is that stuff?" she asked.

"It's called Ekktor," the nurse replied as she rubbed Bea's arm with antiseptic, then prepared to insert a catheter into a vein.

"Yes, but what does it do?" Bea asked.

"It's going to replace Ichor eventually. When they've got it right. Now hold still."

"What's wrong with it now?" Bea asked.

The nurse shook her head impatiently. "I only follow orders," she replied. With that, she inserted the catheter and connected the drip.

Almost instantly the room full of beds disappeared. Instead, Bea found herself out of doors in a place she did not recognize. She was standing in a long line of people, many of whom were fellow volunteers. From somewhere in the distance came a wailing sound, as though hundreds of people were moaning with pain.

Most of those in front of her were staring blankly ahead as if their spirits had been utterly broken. A few others, like herself, were looking around in confusion, trying to take in their surroundings. But no one dared to speak, for they were being watched intently by a dreadful creature in the shape of a man but with a pair of leathery wings sticking out from its shoulder blades. The creature was covered in slime, and in its hand it carried a long, savage-looking whip. From time to time it brought the end of this whip cracking down on the ground to demonstrate that it meant business.

"Where are we?" Bea whispered to the man in front of her.

He gave not the slightest indication that he had heard her. However, the creature with the leathery wings glared furiously in her direction. "Silence!" it shouted in a voice that was even more hideous than its appearance. The whip bit into the ground only inches from where Bea stood.

The sky above her was a livid purple, lit up by slashes of forked lightning. Beneath her feet the earth was deep red, almost the color of blood, and at her back stood a dense forest in which nothing appeared to move. As the line shuffled slowly forward, the moaning grew gradually louder.

Other volunteers began to appear in the line behind Bea. One minute there would be no one there; the next another new recruit would be looking around in bewilderment. They would open their mouths to speak, but then, catching sight of the winged creature with the whip, they would decide to hold their tongues.

Bea could see now that the ground upon which they were standing came to a sudden end up ahead and in its place was a chasm so vast she could not make out the other side. Nevertheless, despite the unimaginable distance involved, it was clear that a bridge was being built out into the abyss. Now she realized where she was. This was the scene she had witnessed when she had stood beside Tzavinyah in the Resurrection Fields and gazed through the telescope at the other side of the abyss.

She recalled what Tzavinyah had told her, that this bridge was the work of their enemy and that it must not be allowed to succeed.

But how could she stop it?

There seemed to be no building materials of any kind. Just the volunteers and a handful of the winged creatures standing around brandishing their whips to make sure no one decided to step out of line. The closer she got to where the work was being carried out, the louder the sound of wailing became.

Then suddenly she saw Dante standing beside the bridge. It was clear that he was the one in charge, the one to whom the winged creatures deferred.

But this was not the Dante who had been her friend. This was the one who had tried to strangle her on the cliff top, the one who had declared himself ruler of Gehenna. So who *was* this person who looked exactly like her friend?

Tzavinyah's warning came back to her: "The bridge that you see is the work of Orobas. He is our enemy, yours and mine and every living creature's. His name means hunger and that is all he is—an appetite that can never be satisfied. He must be stopped, and you are the one who must do it."

One by one the volunteers stepped out onto the bridge and made their way slowly forward, but the moment they reached the edge, they were transformed, becoming merely more stones in the bridge itself. Every stone, she realized, had once been a person. If you looked hard enough, you could see their faces, imprisoned within the masonry and contorted with pain. It was from these stones that the wailing was coming, a testimony to the torment of the volunteers.

Why on earth had Tzavinyah believed she could do anything to prevent this from happening? She had no special powers. She was not even particularly strong. All she had ever possessed was a flickering candle of hope.

As she was thinking this, she became aware that some sort of disturbance was taking place behind her. She turned her head and saw that two people had emerged from the forest. One of them was a youth about her own age. There was an openness about his expression that was completely out of place in this environment. Despite this, he carried a huge knife in one hand. The other was an older man, tall and thin with long white hair and bushy eyebrows. Unlike the volunteers, the two newcomers moved freely, walking briskly in the direction of the bridge, as if they had come to this place by choice.

The winged creatures glanced uncertainly from the newcomers to Dante, waiting for their instructions. Catching sight of Dante, the youth stopped in his tracks.

"Luther!" he cried. Then he shook his head. "No, it can't be. Luther is a thorn tree now. But if you aren't Luther, then why do you look so much like him?"

If Bea could do nothing else, she could at least prevent these two new arrivals from sharing the fate of the volunteers. "His name is Orobas," she called out. "He is the enemy of every living thing! Run!"

But Nyro did not run. Ignoring the sumara running towards him, he took careful aim with the knife and hurled it in the direction of Orobas.

To Nyro's amazement, the knife found its mark, sinking into Orobas's left shoulder. Everyone seemed to hold their breath: the long line of beaten-looking individuals, the sumara that supervised them, the girl who had shouted out the warning, Osman standing beside him, even Nyro himself. For something quite inexplicable seemed to be happening to Orobas. Around the wound that the knife had made, a dark stain was beginning to gather, but it was not made by blood. Instead, it was as if the very substance of his body was changing. Within the darkness of the stain, Nyro glimpsed shapes and symbols that moved and changed, like creatures viewed beneath a microscope. Now the stain began to grow, spreading along Orobas's arm and across his chest so that it seemed likely that it would soon reach out to cover his whole body.

The last part of him to be transformed was his face, but at last this, too, was overtaken until what stood before them no longer resembled anything human except in outline. It still possessed arms, legs, a head and a body, but it was like a living shadow and within its depths the darkness writhed and seethed.

When the knife had first struck home, Nyro had felt a wild surge of triumph. Now, however, he saw that far from wounding his enemy, he had only made it stronger. The creature seemed to have grown in height until it towered above the terrified spectators. Turning to the sumara, it spoke. "Bring them to me! And the girl, too!"

A moment later both Nyro and Osman were seized and dragged towards their enemy, along with Bea. They were taken to the wailing bridge, and Nyro gasped at the vast distance that the bridge was intended to span. Millions upon millions of individuals would be sacrificed before that could be possible.

"Walk!" came the command in a voice that was like stones grinding against each other deep in the bowels of the earth.

Nyro tried with all his strength to resist that order, but despite his best efforts, he found himself placing one foot upon the bridge, and the pain he experienced was unlike anything he had ever known. Yet he still kept walking, for he was no longer in control of what he did. This was the end, he realized. He would never see his parents again. They wouldn't even know what had happened to him. He would not swim in the sea or feel the sun on his skin or the rain lashing his face. He would never laugh or cry or shout or whisper, never have a sweetheart or a job. Still, he kept walking because he had to. Until he reached the very edge of the bridge.

Bea watched them go—first the boy and then the man. Then the creature pointed in her direction, and she felt her feet begin to take her towards the bridge. The moaning of those imprisoned within its masonry was almost deafening now. One more step and she would join them.

Then suddenly everything changed. The world around her rippled and was gone. She was lying in a bed and someone was calling her name.

"Bea, you have to wake up!"

It was her father's voice.

"Come on, Bea, concentrate!"

"What's happening?" she mumbled.

"I disconnected the drip," her father told her. "I can't be a part of this anymore."

She sat up groggily and stared at him in astonishment. "Have you stopped taking Ichor?" she asked.

He frowned. "What are you talking about?"

"Have you stopped taking Ichor?"

"No."

"And yet you disobeyed orders. That must have been so hard!"

"Bea, we haven't got time for this," he told her. "You have to get out of here *now*. When they find out about this, they'll try to kill you!"

Bea nodded. She was properly awake now, though she still felt very weak. "What about you?" she demanded.

He shook his head. "I'm finished."

"No, you're not," she told him. "You're coming with me."

He looked as if he did not dare to believe this might be possible. "But where would I go?" he demanded.

"Let me worry about that!" she told him, grabbing his hand.

LOOKING AT THE STARS

They began by disconnecting all the patients from the drips. "It's probably already too late for them," her father pointed out. But Bea was insistent.

Then her father led the way out of the building. Each time they walked past a security guard, Bea expected to be arrested. But no one took any notice of them. They left through a rear exit that gave onto a paved yard. Now that they were in the open air, her father looked around uncertainly, and Bea could see that the meaning of what he had done was beginning to dawn on him. In a moment he would begin having second thoughts.

In one corner of the yard a motorcycle was parked. Incredibly, the key had been left in the ignition. "Have you ever driven a motorbike?" Bea asked.

"I had one when I was at medical school," her father replied.

"Well then, what are we waiting for?"

Her father looked shocked. "Are you suggesting we steal it?"

"You'd rather stay here and get shot?"

Just then an alarm began ringing inside the medical center. They got on the bike and her father started it up. But then the engine coughed, backfired and died.

Glancing over her shoulder, Bea saw the rear doors to the building opening and a security guard stepping outside.

"It needs more choke," her father said.

"Hurry!" she urged him.

The security guard had spotted them now. He yelled but at the same time the bike's engine roared into life and they shot off around the side of the building.

For a brief moment Bea felt exuberant. But they still had to get past the perimeter fence, and there was the exit looming ahead of them. Two guards stood in front of it, barring the way, while two more were getting ready to close the gates. Recalling her father's earlier doubts, Bea fully expected him to bring the bike to a halt. Instead, he accelerated, driving straight at the guards. They stood there, wide-eyed until the last minute, then leapt aside as Bea and her father hurtled through the gate.

They focused on putting as many miles as possible between themselves and the security guards. As they drove, Bea relived her experience in the Nakara, struggling to make sense of it all. The youth and the old man who had turned up out of the forest—who were they? Why were they not listless and subdued like the other volunteers? But no matter how she puzzled over it, she could not fit the pieces together to make a complete picture.

They rode through a countryside scarred with spoil heaps from abandoned Ichor mines, staying away from settlements wherever possible. At any moment Bea expected to hear the sound of pursuit, but as the hours passed, she began to allow herself to hope that they had succeeded in escaping. By late afternoon they were running low on gasoline and facing a choice of either ditching the motorcycle or going into a town to look for fuel. Then they had a stroke of luck. Riding through a deserted mining village, they spotted a garage. It was shut up and abandoned, but when they broke in and searched the building, they discovered a stack of fuel cans. Bea's father filled up the bike's gas tank. Then they went searching for something to eat.

In a cottage next door to the garage they found three ancient tin cans that had lost their labels. When Bea's father succeeded in opening them with a screwdriver he found in the motorcycle basket, they turned out to contain peaches. It wasn't exactly a feast but it was better than nothing.

By this time the sun was setting, so they decided to spend the night in the cottage and set off again at first light.

"They're bound to catch up with us," Bea's father said. Now that he was no longer busy searching for food, his fears were beginning to reassert themselves.

"Then we'd better find ourselves weapons of some kind," Bea replied.

"Weapons!" Her father looked horrified.

"I know, Dad," Bea said. "We were supposed to have left all that behind. No crime, no violence, no weapons. But the violence was still happening. It was just hidden, wasn't it? What do you think was going on in the dreadful place we've just escaped from?"

"But that was just a mistake," her father objected.

Bea shook her head. "You know that isn't true, don't you?" she said.

He hesitated. Then, slowly, he nodded his head.

Suddenly Bea had an idea. "Bottles!" she said, springing to her feet.

Her father looked confused.

"We need to find some empty bottles," she told him. "And rags. And some matches. Come on, let's start searching before it gets too dark to see anything."

The rags were easy enough. More than one cottage still had curtains hanging, and they found four empty bottles in one of the backyards. But the matches were much more difficult. They were on the point of giving up when Bea's father found a box with three live matches inside. They brought their booty back to the garage, where they filled the bottles with gasoline. Then they tore the curtains into strips and stuffed them into the necks of the bottles. When they were finished, they had a collection of homemade bombs. There was still a great deal of gasoline left and plenty of curtain material, but no more bottles.

Now there was nothing left to do except move the bike around to the back of the garage where it was less obvious, then sit outside and watch the stars come out. It was a cloudless night, which meant that it soon got cold, but neither of them wanted to go in. The night sky was just too beautiful.

"There's the Chariot and Horses," Bea said, pointing to a large cluster of stars in the center of the sky. "I have to say it doesn't look much like a chariot to me."

"The names of the constellations haven't always been the same," her father replied. "The ancient people of Gehenna used to call the Chariot and Horses the Sleeping Giant. Did you know that?"

The Sleeping Giant! The mural on the meetinghouse wall!

"Do you know why they called it that?" Bea asked.

"Well, there isn't much known about those people," her father told her. "There was something about a giant called Enil who created the world by ringing a bell."

There had been a bell beside the giant in the mural!

"What else is in the story?" Bea asked eagerly.

"Let's see. After he created the world, he fell asleep and was forgotten, but they believed that one day he would be woken by the ringing of the same bell, and when he was, the world would end. It's a myth, of course, and myths are one of the things that we aren't supposed to talk about anymore, for some reason." He began pointing out how the shape of the giant could be made out of the stars, but Bea was thinking about the mural and the words of the Mendini Canticle:

> *When every other hope has fled,*
> *When he is lost who once was found,*

Climb the stairs and greet the dawn,
Make the world's most ancient sound.

Suddenly it occurred to her that the second line could refer to Dante. He had been found by Ezekiel in the asylum of Tarnagar and brought to live among the Púca. But now he was lost again. "What do you think—" she started to ask.

But her father interrupted her. "Listen!" he said.

In the distance the sound of motor vehicles could clearly be heard, growing steadily louder.

Her father looked terrified. "What shall we do, Bea?" he asked.

"Get inside the garage and wait," Bea said. "Even if they come this way, they'll probably just drive straight through."

So Bea and her father waited in the garage, making sure that the bombs were within easy reach. Unfortunately, a convoy of trucks pulled up on the outskirts of the village. Dozens of security guards with flashlights got out and began searching the buildings one by one.

"Okay," Bea said when it became clear that they could not just lie low, "this is what we're going to do: wait until they get closer, then throw the bombs. Aim for the trucks. We need to put them out of action if we can."

She began tearing the leftover curtain material into strips, which she then tied together and soaked in gasoline, laying a long fuse from the rear door of the garage to the pile of unused gas cans. She unscrewed the caps of all the cans and put the end of the fuse in one of them.

By now the security guards were only a few doors away. If Bea waited any longer, it would be too late. She struck a match, but it was old and damp and refused to ignite. She tried again but the match broke in half.

"Hurry, Bea!" her father urged her.

"I'm doing my best!" she hissed.

She took out another match and struck it against the side of the box. It flared for an instant, then died. Biting her lip, she picked up the last match. This one had to work. She struck it once. Nothing. Twice. Still nothing.

"They're getting closer," her father whispered.

A third time she struck the match and finally it flared into life. Desperately she cupped the tiny flame with her hand while her father held out two of the bombs and lit the fuses.

"Throw them!" she ordered.

He ran out into the street and flung the bottles in the direction of the security guards. They hit the ground and burst into flame. Meanwhile, Bea lit the other two, and with the burning end of one, she ignited the fuse to the pile of gasoline cans.

When she stepped outside, the night was full of angry shouting and lit up by two pools of burning gasoline. But her father's aim had not been good. The bottles had shattered harmlessly on the ground some distance away from the trucks. She had to do better than that.

The nearest truck was parked a long way down the street. Bea threw the first bottle as hard as she could. It arced through the night sky, then landed in an explosion of flame a couple of yards short. "Damn!" She had been trying too hard. She had to relax a little, forget the security guards who were edging towards her and the fact that the gasoline bomb might explode in her hand at any second, ignore the even bigger bomb in the garage whose fuse was steadily shortening. Instead, she must put all of herself into the action of throwing, so that she became one with the target. She leaned back and her arm swung through a hundred and eighty degrees. The bottle sailed through the air and she saw the security guards' heads turn as they watched it go. It landed directly on the truck, which was instantly engulfed in flames.

She turned to her father. "Follow me!" she said.

There was only one way to reach the motorbike, and that led straight through the garage. As they ran, Bea glanced at the stack of gas cans and saw that the flames were practically licking at its foot.

Her father burst through the rear door to the garage and she followed breathlessly. He leapt onto the bike, kicking it into life in one movement. She climbed on behind him and they sped off into the night. Seconds later the garage exploded. For a terrible moment she felt the hot fingers of death reaching out to grasp them, and she thought they had waited too long. But her father opened the throttle, the bike roared in response and the chaos receded behind them.

THE LIZARD'S MOUTH

It was Seersha's turn to cook the evening meal, and she was sitting outside the hut that she shared with Malachy, peeling the last of the potatoes. The years she had spent working in the kitchen of the Museum of the Leader had taught her how to make a small amount of food go a long way. But even with all her skill, it was getting harder and harder to feed the Púca.

"Soon Dante, or Sigmundus the Second, or whoever is in charge now, won't need to worry about defeating us," she thought gloomily. "Hunger will do the job for him."

The dog Bea had rescued from Podmyn came trotting up to her, sniffing the air eagerly and looking hopefully up at her with his big brown eyes.

"Sorry, Moon," Seersha told him. "I've got nothing for you."

She had christened him Moon because of the little crescent of white fur on his neck. Otherwise, he was completely black.

Moon took no notice of her declaration. Instead, he put his two front paws on her chest and tried to lick her hand.

He was only a puppy, and she could not bring herself to be cross with him. But what on earth had Bea been thinking, bringing them another mouth to feed?

"I should never have let her join those other poor fools, who are almost certainly volunteering for their own deaths," she told herself. But the truth was that nobody could stop Bea once her mind was made up. Her face, as she had announced her intention to join the Faithful, had worn the same look as it had on the day Seersha discovered her in the kitchen of the Museum of the

Leader, making preparations for her escape. Terrified but unstoppable. That was the kind of person she was.

As Seersha was thinking this, she became aware of the sound of an engine in the distance. Albigen came rushing over to her. "There's a motorcycle making its way up the mountain," he said.

"Is it security guards?"

"We don't know yet. Get inside the hut and stay there. We'll take care of them, whoever they are."

So it was that when Bea and her father finally reached the stone huts on the evening after their flight from the blazing garage, they found themselves surrounded by a grim-faced group of armed fighters led by Albigen. But when the Púca saw who was riding on the passenger seat, and when Bea introduced her father, their faces broke into smiles and they all crowded around her. Even the dog refused to be left out, racing around in circles and barking his head off.

Laughing, Bea begged them to calm down. Then, as a cup of tea was handed to her and another put in her father's hand, she told them everything that had happened. But as she described her flight from the burning garage, the smiles faded from their faces.

"Then the security guards may be right behind you," Albigen said.

"I think we lost them," Bea said. "We've seen no one all day."

"Maybe you lost them," Albigen said, "or maybe they just want you to think that."

"I know you believe I shouldn't have gone in the first place, Albigen," Bea said, "but I *have* found out something very important."

"What is it?"

Bea hesitated. "I don't exactly know yet. But it has something to do with the picture of the Sleeping Giant on the wall of the meetinghouse. I need time to work it out."

She could tell from the looks on the faces of her audience that they were unconvinced.

"Albigen's right, Bea," Seersha said gently. "You could easily have been followed here. We'll have to leave this place as soon as we can."

Bea shook her head. "The rest of you can go," she said. "I'm staying here until I've worked out what I have to do."

"Are you sure you know what you're doing, Bea?" her father asked as she left the Púca discussing the next day's traveling arrangements and made her way towards the meetinghouse.

She shook her head. "I'm far from sure." Then she grinned. "But that's never stopped me before. Come on, you have to see this."

She led the way to the mural. It was exactly as she remembered, its vivid colors glowing in the last of the evening sunshine that filtered through the open roof of the building. She glanced at her father and saw the wonder in his eyes. Then they both sat in silence, gazing.

"Why do I think that this mural, the Canticle and the legend are all meant for me?" Bea asked herself. It was just a feeling somewhere deep within her. That and Tzavinyah's prophecy. But what was she supposed to do with this feeling? All she could do was stare at the picture in the hope that a clue might present itself to her.

And then it did.

There was something odd about the lizard in the mural. She rose and walked up close to examine it. From here it was quite obvious that the stone on which the lizard's mouth had been painted protruded slightly from the wall, whereas all the others were completely flush. She touched it and found that it was loose. Perhaps the cement that held it in place had simply crumbled with the passage of time? Or perhaps it was meant to be like that?

She worked the stone back and forth until eventually it came free. Behind it was a dark space.

Her father was standing beside her now, curious to see what she had discovered. "Well, go on then," he said. "Put your hand in."

She reached into the space and immediately her hand touched something cold and smooth.

"What is it?" her father asked.

She felt it all over, her excitement rising. Then she brought it out, taking great care not to let the clapper strike the dome. "Enil's bell!" she announced.

She took it to show the others. "I think I'm meant to climb to the top of the pillar at dawn and ring it," she told them.

"And what's going to happen then?" Albigen asked.

"You remember how Ezekiel once said the Odyll was alive?"

Albigen nodded.

"So couldn't the Sleeping Giant and the Odyll be the same thing?"

"Perhaps," Albigen agreed. "I've never really understood about the Odyll. But if it doesn't work, we leave as soon as it's light enough. It's too dangerous to stay here any longer."

That night Bea lay stretched out on the floor of the hut she shared with Maeve. They had stayed up late into the night talking about the discovery of the bell, what it might mean and what the future of the Púca might be. Now Bea was completely exhausted but still too keyed up to sleep. For all their talking, she still felt as if she did not fully understand what was happening. Yet at the same time, deep within herself, she felt certain that she had been meant to find the bell, and that tomorrow morning when she climbed the pillar and rang it, something truly momentous would happen.

In another hut, lying on the hard stony ground, her father wondered what on earth he had done, then reminded himself that it was too late for such thoughts. Whatever Bea had in mind, he was a part of it now, whether he liked it or not.

Even Moon seemed touched by the Púca's troubles. As he slept in his basket, his legs twitched and he whined quietly to himself, as if he sensed that out there in the night something dangerous was lurking and getting steadily closer with every passing hour.

Night had also fallen upon the mountain of the satsumballa, but not one bird moved so much as a feather. For the Great Flock, time had ceased entirely. All that mattered was that they had been granted a vision of the Hidden Path.

Soon they would set forth on their last great migration; soon they would return to a world in which they truly belonged. For many of them, belief and hope had almost died. They had begun to whisper that perhaps there really was no Hidden Path, that perhaps it was just a story told to chicks as they lay curled up in their nest. But now the evidence was there before them. Amid the rolling billows of the Sky Beyond the Sky lay the start of the Hidden Path, and the giddim had led them there.

Now the Great Flock was ready, its mind made up. Let us go, it sang. Let us delay no longer. The giddim consented. The last flight of the zimbir had begun.

But suddenly everything changed. The Hidden Path grew dim and the music of the Great Flock ceased as a dark figure stepped out of the rolling clouds. It was in the shape of a man but its body was composed of nothing but symbols of enormous power and pitiless cruelty.

"Dante Cazabon!" said the voice of Orobas. "Don't tell me you're planning to disappear altogether when you and I have so much unfinished business to complete!"

Frustration and fury replaced the excitement Dante had been feeling. He wanted to leave his past behind him and take the Hidden Path with the rest of the flock. "Why can't you leave me alone?" he demanded. "You've got my body. Isn't that enough for you?"

"There is never enough for me," Orobas told him. "You must know that by now. I want everything, Dante. Your mind as well as your body. That's the most interesting part, after all. There's so much pleasure to be got from it."

With these words he stretched out his arm and pointed at Kidu's chest. Immediately Dante felt the bird grow cold and he realized that the same corrupt symbols that made up Orobas's phantom had infected Kidu. As the bird watched helplessly, the symbols grew bigger—and it was clear that before long they would overwhelm him completely.

"Help me, Giddim!" Kidu urged.

Dante struggled to fight the corruption, but it was far too strong for him. It was as though he were trapped in a narrow cavern deep underground and cold water was rising all around him. It seemed that Orobas had finally succeeded in defeating him.

Then suddenly he felt a slackening of the creature's will.

"No!" Orobas whispered. "It cannot be!"

"What cannot be?" Dante wondered. Something of enormous significance must be taking place, something that Orobas had not counted upon.

"I will not allow it!" Orobas roared, and his proclamation seemed to drown out everything else.

A moment later the Great Flock was back upon the slopes of the mountain, Kidu and Dante with them. They had been cast out of the Odyll and thrown back to earth as carelessly as one might toss a pebble. Relief filled Dante, but in his mind an image remained, confused yet urgent, like the remnants of a dream.

During those last moments he had spent within the Odylic realm, his mind had been so nearly joined to Orobas's mind that he had shared his enemy's last thought. What had caused his enemy such distress? Dante struggled to bring the vision into focus. Something to do with a bell?

Meanwhile, the Chief Buzzard stared fixedly at Kidu with his one bloodshot eye, and every other bird in the Great Flock waited to see what he would say.

"Kidu Kekkaka," he began at last. "Though many here doubted you, myself included, your gïddim did indeed show us the Hidden Path as you promised. We will always wish in our hearts that he did not turn back from the brink. Yet perhaps there was no other choice. For what we have seen, we thank you."

He bowed slightly and Kidu bowed in reply.

"It is the decision of the satsumballa, therefore," the Chief Buzzard continued, "that you be allowed to go free. But more than that, I declare that you are the Zimbir That Is Not Zimbir. The Great Flock is yours to command."

As Kidu looked around in astonishment, a great chorus of squawks and chirps and whistles and bird cries of every kind greeted the announcement.

"We great now," the bird said delightedly, speaking inside his mind. "We in charge. We heroes, Kidu and Giddim."

But there was no time for congratulations. The chaotic set of impressions with which Orobas had left Dante had finally resolved into a clear picture, and he understood at last that Bea was in terrible danger.

"What we do next, Giddim?" Kidu demanded.

"Fly, Kidu," Dante urged him. "Fly like you never flew before!"

THE SUMMONER

It was still dark when Bea woke, but she could tell by the stars that dawn was not far away. She dressed quickly and, with the bell clutched tightly in her hand, stepped outside, taking care not to wake Maeve.

She had not gone very far when the night was suddenly illuminated. Blinded by the light, she stopped in her tracks.

"Stay where you are!" a voice ordered.

The huts were surrounded by security guards. They had trained a spotlight on her, and one of them was speaking through a megaphone. Squinting against the light, Bea saw that there were dozens of them holding guns pointed directly at her, while others were dragging the sleeping Púca from their huts.

"Albigen was right," Bea thought. "I led them straight here."

Two of the guards stepped forward and seized her arms. Then out of the shadows stepped Dante—or Sigmundus the Second, as he now appeared to be.

Even with the light shining directly in her eyes, Bea could see that there was something terribly wrong with him. His face looked as though it were covered with tattoos, but as Bea stared more closely, she saw that the tattoos were alive, that they moved across his face as though they were insects that lived beneath his skin.

"What has happened to you, Dante?" she cried out.

He lifted his arm and pointed to the bell. "Take the Summoner from her and bring it to me," he ordered in a voice entirely devoid of any emotion.

Bea held on as firmly as she could, kicking at the guard's legs as he began prying the bell from her fingers. One by one, he peeled her fingers back.

Suddenly, without warning, the sky above them thronged with shadowy forms and the air was full of the sound of birdcalls. Birds dropped down upon the beehive huts in their thousands as if the sky were raining feathers. Straight at Sigmundus the Second and the security guards they came, tearing at their faces with razor-sharp claws, stabbing at their eyes with beaks like knives. In a moment their victims disappeared under swarms of feathered attackers, and still more came all the time.

Free of her captors and still clutching the bell, Bea raced across the stony ground towards the pillar. The dawn was already knocking on the door of the world.

Panting, she reached the base of the pillar only to find that her way was blocked. Standing in front of her was a young man whom she recognized, yet did not recognize. A memory that had been buried deep within a dream began to surface.

"I see you were not expecting me," the young man said with a smile of unspeakable cruelty. "Don't tell me you've forgotten your promise."

"Set!" she said, as her recollection of the dream finally crystallized.

He nodded. "You may call me that."

"I have to climb this pillar," she told him, glancing skyward. Surely it was beginning to grow perceptibly lighter in the east?

"You needn't worry about that anymore," Set said. "You're mine now. I will make you queen of the Nakara. Just think of that!"

"I don't want to be queen of anywhere!" Bea told him.

"Too late! Remember your promise—when the sky is full of

feathers and the moon sleeps in a basket. A girl should always keep her promises, you know."

"But if I don't . . . ," Bea began.

"If you don't ring the bell, Orobas will be victorious." Set finished the sentence for her. "Of course. But that is no longer your concern."

"But why?" Bea asked. "Why do you want to stop me?"

"Because this is my world," Set replied, "and I am its lord. You didn't know that, did you? Your ancestors believed in me but that was long ago, and as the years went by, you all forgot my name. The birds did not forget, however. They called me Shurruppak and they never ceased to fear me. Orobas, too, was careful to respect me. He placed himself under my protection and he was wise to do so. For I am all that stands in the way of his destruction. But I *do* stand in the way. For if I let you ring that bell, it would mean my destruction, too. So I will not allow it."

He reached out his hand. "Give me the Summoner," he ordered.

But then another voice spoke, a voice like the sound of bells ringing out across a landscape of snow and ice. "Step aside, brother," it said.

Bea turned and saw that Tzavinyah was standing beside her. Her heart was filled with a wild joy, even as anger flashed from Set's eyes. "You have no business interfering!" he cried.

"I have every business," Tzavinyah told him. "I am here to ensure that the summons is issued."

Set raised his left hand in the air with the palm facing outwards, and a ray of light shot out towards Tzavinyah. The air around Bea grew so hot that she felt as if her hair might burn up, but immediately Tzavinyah raised his right arm in a similar gesture. From his palm there came a similar beam of power, though this one seemed to chill the air so that Bea shivered as she watched. The twin forces met in the middle and locked so that for a time the two brothers stood there, arms raised above their heads in a duel, until at last Set lowered his arm and his beam vanished.

Tzavinyah followed suit. "There is no difference in strength between us," he conceded. "Only Bea can decide which of us will prevail."

Bea was about to open her mouth and say that she would choose Tzavinyah when Set spoke first. "Consider this before you make your decision," he said. "If you give me the bell and come with me, all of this will be like a dream. In its place I will conjure up a world that is tailor-made for you, a world that contains every pleasure and diversion you can possibly imagine. But if you choose Tzavinyah, you choose death."

"What do you mean?" Bea asked.

"When you ring the bell, it will not just be the end for Orobas," Set continued. "You, too, will die. And death will mean the end of everything. For make no mistake, by ringing that bell you will wake the Odyll—and once that has happened, there will be no Resurrection Fields for those who have died."

Bea hesitated. She had not thought about what might happen if she rang the bell, at least not beyond the notion that it might somehow bring about the defeat of Orobas. But she had always assumed she would survive, along with all her friends.

She looked at Tzavinyah. "Is it true?" she asked.

But Tzavinyah only looked back at her without speaking. His expression was unfathomable.

"He does not know," Set told her. "The answer is hidden from him, like so much else. But I have looked in places he will not contemplate. I have turned every page in every forbidden book that was ever written. I have sifted through the ruin that time has made of the world, lifted every stone and gazed underneath. That is why

I know what comes after the ringing of the bell, and I promise you it is the end of everything."

Bea glanced up at the sky. There could be no mistake now. It was definitely growing brighter in the east. "And if I do not ring it?" she asked.

"Then Orobas will triumph," Tzavinyah replied quietly.

It was all very well to pretend you were not afraid of death, Bea thought, but people only said that because they had not truly looked death in the eye. They had not understood that it meant everything you had always taken for granted and loved without even knowing it—the world around you, the memories you carry with you, your hopes for the future—all of this being extinguished like a candle flame that is blown out. And afterwards, there would be nothing. Not even emptiness. Not even loneliness. Not even pain.

Bea didn't want that. She couldn't bear it. "I am still so young," she thought, and a single tear ran down her cheek.

But then she took a deep breath and began to climb the steps. At the top of the pillar she gazed out at the edge of the world, where the yellow lip of the sun was just beginning to emerge above the horizon. Slowly she held out her arm, and with a trembling hand, she rang the bell.

The sound started off very small, so that she wondered if she had made some sort of mistake. But instead of dying away, the peal of the bell grew louder and louder still until it seemed as if it would drown the whole world in sound. At the same time, Bea saw her own life played out before her mind's eye, unwinding like a film playing backwards, slowly at first, then faster and faster until it was a kaleidoscope of images and then finally a blur that faded into white light.

EPILOGUE

Bea was standing in the middle of a vast, grassy plain. Here and there a few trees dotted the landscape, and a small white bird flew across the sky. She knew she should recognize this place, but there was a blurriness to everything, almost as if she were looking at something underwater. Then it came to her: these were the Resurrection Fields. Not far away, the ground suddenly began to move. A shower of earth was flung upwards, and a human hand pushed through the soil, then another, followed by a man's head. With a little difficulty, the owner of the head clambered out of the hole he had just made. He was white-haired, a little stooped and completely naked. He looked mildly dazed and completely unaware that he was being watched. This did not surprise Bea, nor did she feel in the least embarrassed. In fact, she had the distinct feeling that she was not really there at all but looking on from a distance, and that she was quite invisible to the white-haired man. There was something familiar about him, but no matter how hard she tried, Bea could not recall where she had seen him before. After a little while he seemed to pull himself together, and with a sudden smile he began walking away from her.

Before she could see where he went, another figure began digging himself out. This time it was a boy of about her own age. Once again Bea was not uncomfortable about seeing him emerge naked since she was quite sure that was how it was meant to be. Once again she had the feeling that she almost recognized him, but she could not think of his name. The boy looked about him and grinned delightedly. Then he walked off in the direction that the white-haired man had already taken.

As she watched him go, everything began clouding over and Bea felt a kind of dizziness come over her, so that she thought she might be sick at any moment. At the same time she realized that her thoughts were disappearing, leaving nothing in their place. She struggled to remember what she had been thinking about just a moment ago. Was it something about a man? Or a boy? But it was no good. It was as if someone had taken the contents of her mind and shaken them out into the wind. She felt a brief moment of utter panic. What if her thoughts never returned to her again? What if she could not even remember who she was?

The next thing she knew, she was sitting on the branch of a tree, holding a book in her hand. It was her favorite tree, an ancient willow so bent over that its branches grew parallel to the ground, a place where she often came to sit and read.

So what had she been thinking about just a moment ago? She frowned and concentrated as hard as she could, but the answer would not come. It must have been something to do with the story she was reading, but for the life of her, she could not recall it now.

Perhaps it was time to go home. She closed her book and stood up. Then she noticed the boy. He was standing some distance away among the trees, gazing in her direction. He was slim and pale with fair hair and very blue eyes, and there was the hint of a smile on his face. It occurred to her that he was laughing at her, and she felt a wave of indignation.

"What do you think you're doing spying on me?" she demanded, trying to look her most dignified.

"I wasn't spying," the boy replied. "I was just walking along when I saw you."

Bea was not sure that she believed him. This was *her* spot. No one else ever came here. She looked at him more closely. It was on the tip of her tongue to say something rather cutting and put him in his place, but then she stopped herself. After all, he had just as much right to be here as she did. If it came to that, they were both trespassers—the old hospital had been closed to the public for years. She wondered if he had climbed through the same gap in the fence that she had.

Now that she looked at him more closely, she had a distinct feeling that they had met somewhere before. But it was very odd because she also felt quite certain that it had not been in this lifetime.

"My name's Bea," she said. Then she stopped, surprised at herself. What was she doing telling him her name?

"I'm Dante," he replied. "What're you reading?"

She hesitated. But some part of her seemed determined to be friendly, despite her better judgment. She held up the book, and he read the title aloud.

"*The Promises of Dr. Sigmundus*. What's it like?"

She thought about trying to explain the story but then she heard herself say, "I'll lend it to you when I've finished if you like."

"Beatrice Argenti," she thought, "have you taken leave of your senses? He'll think you're throwing yourself at him."

But he just smiled, a proper smile this time. "Thanks very much," he said. "I love a good book."

158

ABOUT THE AUTHOR

Brian Keaney is a celebrated British author of young adult fiction. His writing has earned the admiration of such stellar contemporaries as His Dark Materials' Philip Pullman. Says Pullman of Keaney's *Jacob's Ladder:* "[T]his novel has an original tone and an unusual setting. I applaud Keaney's seriousness of purpose."

The seed for The Promises of Dr. Sigmundus was sown when, at thirteen, Keaney first read Dante's *The Divine Comedy* and became deeply affected by the classic tale's visions and themes.

After his family, writing is Keaney's primary passion. He makes a habit of spending time on a farm in Ireland, "sitting on the hillside, listening to the wind blowing through the heather and letting the stories grow in my mind."

Also Available

The Hollow People

Book One in The Promises of Dr. Sigmundus

The Cracked Mirror

Book Two in The Promises of Dr. Sigmundus

"Brian Keaney's writing is spare and taut and there is never a word out of place or one that doesn't ring true." —*The Times Educational Supplement*